"I wanted to say *danke* to you..."

"For what?" Susanna asked.

"For refusing to give the gossips more fodder about Miriam and me," Seth said.

Her mouth dropped open. "You overheard what was being said in the barn?"

He nodded. "I did. Most of it, I think. And I appreciate your words of support."

He almost smiled at the impudent way she lifted her chin higher in the air.

"Most of those women mean well and have nothing but compassion for what you and Miriam are going through," she said. "But some of them need to be taught a lesson by the Savior's commandment to love one another."

Ducking his head, he silently agreed as he gave his daughter a happy squeeze. The baby smiled and chortled something only she could comprehend.

"It looks like Miriam approves of our agreement, too," he said.

Susanna laughed, the sound high and sweet.

It caused something to soften inside of him... and stirred an emotion he didn't understand.

Leigh Bale is a *Publishers Weekly* bestselling author. She is the winner of the prestigious Golden Heart® Award and was a finalist for the Gayle Wilson Award of Excellence and the Booksellers' Best Award. The daughter of a retired US forest ranger, she holds a BA in history. Married in 1981 to the love of her life, Leigh and her professor husband have two children and two grandkids. You can reach her at leighbale.com.

Visit the Author Profile page at LoveInspired.com for more titles.

An Amish Christmas Wish

Leigh Bale

LOVE INSPIRED
INSPIRATIONAL ROMANCE

LOVE INSPIRED®
INSPIRATIONAL ROMANCE

ISBN-13: 978-1-335-58615-5

An Amish Christmas Wish

Recycling programs
for this product may
not exist in your area.

Love Inspired
22 Adelaide St. West, 41st Floor
Toronto, Ontario M5H 4E3, Canada
www.LoveInspired.com

Printed in U.S.A.

For if ye forgive men their trespasses,
your heavenly Father will also forgive you.
—*Matthew* 6:14

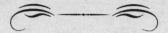

Chapter One

The store was perfect. It would completely suit her needs. Cupping her hands around her eyes to shut out the glare of morning sunlight, Susanna Glick leaned forward and peered through the wide, sparkling windows. The interior of the salesroom looked painfully neat, expansive and empty of merchandise. Just ready and waiting for someone to open a business here.

The crisp autumn air caused her to shiver and she pulled her warm, woolen cloak tighter at her throat. Her breath came out in little puffs of air and immediately formed circles of frost on the glass pane. The late October weather would soon give way to the cold winter months…and then the holidays. Ideal for opening a new shop.

Stepping back, she studied the outside of the building. A fresh coat of white paint and blue trim showed off the frame structure to perfection. A new portico overhead shielded the front entrance from inclement weather. That would be nice for her customers.

Susanna knew Seth Lehman, the owner of the place, had worked hard over the past two years to renovate the ramshackle walls and plumbing. And from what she could see, he'd succeeded brilliantly. The structure's location at the end of Main Street was ideal. Quaint and charming, it was the first store customers would see when they drove into Riverton, Colorado. Hopefully, they would stop and buy her products. Susanna could envision a large, bright sign to draw their attention. Thanksgiving and Christmas were just around the corner. Locals and tourists alike would flock to her store, eager to buy her handmade Amish noodles and other pastas as gifts or to cook for their family gatherings. She just knew it!

Stepping over to the door, she knocked on the portal and cocked an ear to listen for movement inside. When she didn't hear any sounds, she paused, wondering if Seth was home. If he would rent the place to her, she could easily drive her horse and buggy into town from where she lived with her grandmother a mile down the road. Their Amish farm and noodle business kept them busy. But after her abusive husband's death a year earlier, that suited Susanna fine. Because to her, *busy* was synonymous with financial independence and the freedom to never marry and find herself under the control of a domineering man again.

Hmm. Still no answer. She knew Seth and Eve Lehman had lived together in an upstairs apartment with their cute, nine-month-old daughter, Miriam. Like Susanna, they were Amish, though Eve had been shunned for adultery and left town right after Miriam's birth. At church, Susanna had heard enough to know the marriage had not been a happy one. Hushed whispers claimed Eve was addicted to alcohol and illicit drugs. She had also been living with *Englisch* men who weren't her husband. And to the Amish, that was particularly scandalous.

The fact that Eve had been shunned told Susanna there must be some truth to the rampant gossip. The church elders had proposed counseling, but Eve had apparently refused all offers and wouldn't even attend church.

Susanna's heart went out to Seth and little Miriam, who needed a *mamm* to care for her. And Susanna couldn't help wondering who was looking after the baby while Seth worked in the fields of his farm out back.

No one was here. Maybe Seth was in the barn. After all, it was time to harvest potatoes. A killing frost could freeze the ground any day now. Like every other farmer in the area, he'd be outside digging up his spuds. Though there was no farmhouse out back, he had a huge barn and fenced acreage where he grew fields of hay, too. The shorter growing season and cooler temperatures here in Colorado meant they could only grow hay, potatoes and a little barley with much success. Potatoes were a cash crop. Even Susanna had planted two acres of her land into spuds, which helped pay her mortgage. She needed to harvest them soon. But first things first.

She turned, planning to walk around the building to find and speak with Seth. A thin wail drew her attention toward the upper floor. Leaning her cheek against the door, she listened. Yes! There it was again. The unmistakable cry of a baby, coming from the second floor overhead.

Turning the doorknob, Susanna was surprised to find it unlocked. She stepped inside, the pungent scent of pine cleaner making her nose twitch. The hardwood floors and countertops gleamed. An old-fashioned cash register sat at one end of the long front counter. The empty shelves and display cases were just waiting for someone to stock them with products.

The crying grew louder and Susanna crossed the room. As she stepped into a hallway at the back of the store, she saw another door and couldn't resist peeking inside. Much to her delight, the room was a spacious kitchen with an oversize sink, counters, shelves, a table and a large stainless steel island that would be perfect for rolling out dough. Like the outer store, everything was fastidiously scrubbed and ready for occupancy.

The wailing persisted and she stepped over to the staircase.

"Seth! Is anyone here?" she called up, speaking in *Deitsch*, the Germanic language her Amish people used among themselves.

The crying stopped briefly and a fussing sound took its place, then the bawling resumed with intensity.

Glancing at the front door, Susanna thought she should leave right now. After all, she had entered without an invitation.

She turned away, planning to go outside and look for Seth in the fields. But the babe's miserable cries pulled at her heartstrings. What if the child was hurt?

Ascending the stairs to the apartment above, she met a door at the top and knocked again.

"Seth! It's Susanna Glick. Are you here?" she asked.

The crying ceased abruptly and she could hear the baby snuffling. When she didn't go inside, the howling continued.

She turned the doorknob and pushed the panel open before peering inside.

"Seth? *Hallo?*" she called for good measure.

The room was small, combining a kitchenette and living area into one with a dining table that would accommodate no more than four people. A leather bridle lay across the narrow counter and the sink was filled with dirty dishes. Buried beneath a pile of soiled laundry, a plain brown sofa sat against the far wall. A basket filled with freshly washed diapers rested on the floor with a stack nearby to indicate someone had started folding them.

Little Miriam stood inside her playpen, wearing a filthy lavender dress and white apron that matched the same plain Amish style Susanna wore. The baby's feet were bare, her face red, and her tiny body trembled with the impact of her tears.

Upon seeing Susanna, Miriam cried out and lifted her tiny arms as she gave a pitiful sound of relief. The child's eyes held such a sad, pleading look that Susanna could not deny her anything. Not at that moment.

"*Hallo, Liebchen.* Where's your *daed*?" Susanna asked in a sympathetic tone as she glanced around.

She stepped over to the playpen and picked up the girl, holding her close against her chest. Miriam immediately released a shuddering sigh of ease. Her hair and clothes smelled of sour milk. Her diaper was wet and Susanna cooed and talked to her as she quickly changed the girl before picking her up again. Content to finally be in someone's arms, Miriam rested her cheek against Susanna's chest, gave a shuddering exhale and sucked her fingers. Susanna's heart gave a powerful squeeze. She'd always wanted a child of her own but realized that would never happen now. She would rather die than remarry and find herself being dictated to by another brutal man. It was that simple. And so, there would never be any children for her. But for some reason, that thought made Susanna's heart ache like never before.

Pushing the pile of dirty clothes aside, she sat on the sofa and comforted the baby, wondering when she had eaten last. The Amish raised large families and always helped one another with their kids. Susanna knew what to do. She just wasn't sure she wanted to go digging around in the kitchen to find milk and a clean bottle.

"There, there. What's all this fuss about? And where is your *daed*?" Susanna spoke softly as she rocked Miriam back and forth.

She didn't really expect an answer but thought the sound of her voice might further calm the girl.

In response, Miriam shot out a hand toward the door and babbled something only she could understand. Though Eve, the baby's mother, had been shunned, she could have repented and made things right. Their Amish congregation would have then welcomed Eve back with open arms. Susanna couldn't comprehend how any *mamm* could leave her own child like this. What was so appealing about a life of drugs and alcohol that would induce

Eve to abandon her own baby? Susanna didn't understand the power of addiction. Not at all.

But where was Seth?

Since Susanna didn't know the entire story, she was not in a position to judge. Nor was it her problem. She had come here to speak with Seth about renting the bottom portion of his building so she could open a shop to sell her handmade noodles and other products. And since she never planned to marry again, that meant she must earn enough to provide a living for herself and her elderly grandmother. She did not have time to get embroiled in someone else's woes.

So, where was the guy? Would he be back soon? And why had he left his teeny daughter all alone?

A rattle downstairs and then the slamming of an outer door told her she would soon have an answer. The sounds of boot heels thudded against the stairs, indicating someone was coming up to the apartment. Trying to hide any looks of disapproval, Susanna sat up straight but continued to rock the baby.

The door opened as Seth shouldered his way into the room carrying two buckets of frothy white milk. At first glance, his hazel eyes widened with surprise and he immediately nudged the bridle aside and set the buckets on the counter with a little thump.

"Hallo," she said, her voice sounding a bit frosty to her ears.

"Susanna. I didn't know you were here," he said, whisking the battered black felt hat off his head and tossing it aside.

He wore a plain black coat that had a ripped sleeve but looked warm and practical. His unruly hair was overly long, the color of damp sand. As he stood in the kitchen, his high forehead crinkled in a heavy frown. He shrugged out of the coat, his muscular chest and shoulders filling his white chambray shirt, which was stained by hours of hard work. He gazed at her with tired but intelligent eyes. His short beard with no moustache indicated he was married. Wearing black suspenders, heavy work boots and plain, broadfall pants, he looked every inch the Amish farmer. He was quite handsome, in a rustic sort of way. But since he was married and Susanna had no interest in any man, she looked away. The Amish didn't believe in divorce. Even if Eve never returned, Seth could never remarry as long as the woman was still alive.

"I... I just arrived. I'm sorry to barge in like this, but I heard Miriam crying, so I came to check on her," she said, trying not to sound too disapproving.

He shrugged one powerful shoulder and lifted a calloused hand in a helpless gesture. "She was asleep when I left. I thought I could get the goats and cows milked before she awoke. Apparently I was wrong."

Susanna dropped her mouth open. "But what if there had been a house fire? Or what if she had choked on a toy? It's not safe to leave a young child alone for any length of time…"

She stopped, realizing her comments might be taken as criticism. And right now, she wanted something from this man, which meant she should not irritate him.

He inclined his head. "*Ja*, you are right, of course. I hate to leave her alone. With Eve gone, it… It has been rather difficult to care for a *boppli* on my own."

His words reminded her not to be unkind. She could just imagine the challenging position he was in and the pain he must feel over Eve's abandonment.

"You could hire someone to look after Miriam," she suggested.

He released a sigh of impatience, shook his head and looked down at his booted feet.

Though he didn't explain, she suspected there was more to this story than she realized. She didn't want to know anything about it. She told herself she didn't care. But deep in her heart, she knew that wasn't true.

"I did hire someone but… As I said, it has been rather difficult. What did you need?" he asked with a sigh of resignation.

He came toward her…all six feet two inches of him. Realizing it was not proper for her to be alone with a married man, Susanna stood and moved across the room with Miriam in tow.

Seth stopped and stared after her with wide eyes, as if he had just realized the same thing.

"Why did you *komm* here?" Seth asked again, turning toward the buckets of milk.

He sounded a bit curt and she figured he was tired, hungry and carrying plenty of burdens of his own.

Susanna watched as he made room in the stainless steel sink and set a large, clean bowl there, then poured the milk through a strainer. With him safely across the room, she relaxed a bit, trying to calm her racing heart.

"I… I was wondering if you would be willing to rent the space downstairs to me. I would like to expand my noodle business and open a store before Thanksgiving. With the holiday season upon us, I thought it would be a great time for a grand opening," she said.

There. That was good. Succinct and to the point. The building bordered his farmland out back. Eve, his wife, was an incredible cook. Over a year earlier, she had once told Susanna that she wanted to open a bakery here. But after three years of being married to Seth, that never happened. And with Eve being shunned and gone so long this time, Susanna thought maybe Seth would be happy to have a tenant paying rent to help with his bills. Maybe it would even help him hire childcare for his daughter.

He glanced at Susanna and frowned as a look of grief crossed his face. Oh, that wasn't good. As he opened his mouth to speak, Susanna braced herself for the worst. But a loud knock and then a voice calling from down below stopped him. Someone else was here.

"Excuse me, please." Seth stepped over to the door.

Susanna hurried aside to let him pass, bracing Miriam against her hip. The sounds of heavy feet coming up the stairs filled her ears.

"*Hallo!* Can I help you?" Seth called down.

"Yes, we're looking for Seth Lehman," a deep, male voice said.

"I am Seth."

He stepped back and Susanna almost dropped the baby when two uniformed police officers walked into the room. Susanna had seen the men around town before, though she had never spoken to them. After all, the Amish avoided the *Englisch* and their worldly ways if at all possible.

With gleaming badges on their chests and radios and guns holstered at their sides, the two men looked authoritative and rather imposing. And all of a sudden, Susanna wished she had never approached Seth about renting his store.

"What do you want?" Seth asked the two officers.

He couldn't believe the week he was having. First, Hilda, one of his Percheron draft horses, had thrown a shoe and he had to stop to fix it. Then, the rounded plate on his potato digger broke off and the welder in town couldn't repair it until tomorrow. At this rate, he'd never get his potatoes dug and gathered before a hard freeze set in and he prayed the weather held for at least one more week.

All day long, he'd carried Miriam wrapped warm in a sling on his back as he worked, and she had been as good as gold. Babbling and waving her little arms, pulling his hair with her tiny fists, knocking his hat off and falling asleep when she got tired. He stopped often to check on her, change her diaper and feed her. And every time, she smiled so wide that he had to kiss her sweet face. He didn't have the heart to begrudge such an endearing child. But the fields were no place for a baby. He hadn't found time to wash the laundry, so he hadn't changed Miriam's dress in several days. Soon, it would be too cold to take her with him while he worked. He needed permanent childcare, whether he liked it or not.

Then, the one time he left his sleeping daughter alone while he went to milk the goats, he had returned to find her in the arms of Susanna Glick. Occasionally, he took Miriam to a woman in his congregation to watch her for the day, but most of the Amish farms were located miles outside town. Driving his horse and buggy back and forth was more than inconvenient and sucked up a goodly portion of his day. He would love to hire someone to come here to his home instead but all the girls in his congregation who were ma-ture enough to watch a baby were needed to work on their parents' farms. And most married Amish women had oodles of kids of their own and couldn't spend the day at his place.

Eve's absence had put him in a real bind. But even if she was here, he wouldn't dare leave Miriam alone with her for long. He feared she might take drugs that would put her into a stupor so she couldn't watch the baby properly. Eve had been shunned for her wild behavior. Per the tenets of their *Ordnung*, the unwritten rules his Amish congregation followed, he couldn't eat at the same table with her or take anything from her hand. He could still speak to her but only to use gentle persuasion to convince her to repent and come back home where she belonged. If she softened her angry heart and truly wanted to overcome her addictions, he would do almost anything to help her recover. But she had to want to get clean and sober, first. She had to want to change. It was that simple, and yet that difficult.

Now, he had two policemen standing in his home, filling the room with their badges and guns. And just one thought pounded Seth's mind.

What had Eve done this time?

The older of the two men stepped forward as he jerked a thumb toward his companion. "This is Officer Davies and I'm Officer Walton."

"*Ja*, I know. You've been here before. What can I do for you?" Seth asked.

He wished the officers would leave so he could process the milk and feed Miriam before taking her with him back out to the barn to finish his chores. He didn't need this interruption. Not now. He didn't need more trouble caused by Eve.

Walton's eyes creased with sympathy. "Mr. Lehman…"

"Call me Seth," he said.

The Amish didn't like formalities and preferred being addressed by their given names.

Walton nodded. "Seth… Your wife is Eve Lehman, correct?"

"*Ja*, you already know that," Seth said.

It was as he feared. Eve had done something wrong. Again. Over the past few years, the police had come to his home on several previous occasions. Usually when Eve needed him to bail her out of jail. But no more. Seth had warned her the last time, right before she had been shunned by their congregation, that he wouldn't get her out of trouble again. This time, she needed to face the consequences of her actions on her own.

He had wed his wife almost three years earlier. Both of them were from Indiana. Though he hadn't known her well at the time, he had wanted to love her. He'd tried so much.

Their two families had arranged their marriage. Seeking more affordable property, Seth had moved to Colorado five years ago. With forty acres of fertile land, he'd worked hard and was pleased with the fine farm he'd built. He could support a wife and wanted nothing more than to raise a *familye* of his own. His *mamm* had written to tell him that Eve was an excellent cook. But what no one had told him was that she'd also fallen in with a wild crowd of *Englisch* kids and gotten hooked on alcohol and illicit drugs. He'd discovered too late that her *familye* agreed to the match in hopes a change of scenery would pull her out of her dependence on drugs. Seth had married her and they'd had several weeks of wedded bliss before Eve's addictions reared their ugly heads. And since that time, Seth and Miriam had become the collateral damage in Eve's life.

"What has happened?" Seth asked.

As if sensing her *daed's* morose mood,

Miriam started fretting. Susanna rocked back and forth to settle the baby.

"I'm sorry to bring you such sad news, but Eve died six days ago," Walton said.

Died?! Seth blinked, his ears feeling clogged like they were full of water.

"*Ne*, you're wrong. She couldn't be dead. There's been some mistake," Seth blurted the words.

He couldn't believe it. Couldn't accept it.

Walton frowned, his eyes flickering with compassion. "I'm sorry, Seth. There's been no mistake."

Seth's legs wobbled and he felt suddenly weak. He stepped back, stumbled and plopped down on the sofa before he fell flat on his face. He took a sharp inhale, trying to absorb the awful truth. Eve was gone. Dead. He was now a widower and Miriam was an orphan.

"How... How did it happen?" he asked, conscious of his daughter whimpering.

"The cause of death appears to be a drug overdose, but we won't know for sure until the toxicology tests are completed in another week," Walton said.

The man reached into his shirt pocket and pulled out two business cards, which he handed to Seth. "She's at the hospital morgue in Pueblo. The police contacted us. It'd be best if you went there as soon as possible to identify her body, just to make certain it's really her. As soon as the ME releases her body, you can have her transferred here to Riverton and make burial arrangements."

"What is an ME?" Seth asked, staring at the cards until the words blurred in front of his eyes.

He couldn't believe this was happening. It wasn't true. It couldn't be!

"Medical examiner," Davies said.

Seth nodded, not really focused on what they were saying. All he had ever wanted was a wife and *familye* of his own. To be a normal Amish man with a faithful woman to work beside him and raise lots of children for them to love. Though Eve had been beautiful on their wedding day, she had never been normal. There was too much fire and ice flowing through her veins. Too much anger and rebellion for her to ever live the plain, dutiful life of an Amish woman. To please her, Seth had bought this dilapidated building at a dirt-cheap price. It had taken quite a bit of time but he'd fixed it up, finishing the work six months earlier. He'd kept it dusted and clean, hoping to entice Eve back home to start a bakery here. But his strategy hadn't worked. The store still sat empty and he hadn't seen his wife in almost nine months.

Now, all Seth's hopes and dreams had been dashed on the rocks of disappointment and despair. For some time, he had contemplated selling out and moving back home to Indiana, where his *familye* could help him care for Miriam. But the hope that Eve might return, get off the drugs and finally bc a wife to him and a *mudder* to Miriam had anchored him here in Colorado. That and an innate feeling deep inside his heart that, if he left now, he'd lose more than just his wife and farm. He would also miss out on his last chance for a happy home life.

"Who… Who found her?" Seth asked.

Davies released a quiet exhale. "A dog walker."

Seth jerked and stared at the man. "A dog walker?"

"Yes, she was found in the city park in Pueblo. She was alone, lying in the bushes," Walton said.

Seth swallowed hard. "Are you…are you certain she wasn't ki-killed?"

Walton nodded. "There were no signs of foul play. We don't believe it's a homicide."

So. Eve had been alone in the park, doing drugs. That hurt Seth's feelings like nothing else could. And yet, it was so like her. Going off by herself, hiding out while she lost touch with reality. Forgetting she had a husband and daughter at home who wanted and needed her so much.

"We'll leave you now. If you have any questions, my name and phone number are on one of the cards. Feel free to call me anytime," Walton said.

"I… I don't have a phone," Seth said.

Walton frowned. "Then, you can just walk down to the station. There's always an officer on duty, night and day. And again, I'm sorry for you and your daughter's loss."

His daughter. How he wished Miriam was his child. If they knew the awful truth, they might not be so kind. They might even try to take Miriam away from him. And Seth couldn't let that happen. Not now, not ever.

He watched them leave, watched Susanna close the door quietly behind them. As she faced him, he could see tears shimmering in her expressive eyes. He hated that she was here to witness this shame. And yet, he was also grateful he wasn't alone right now.

Susanna cuddled Miriam close and kissed

the baby's cheek, speaking quietly to her. He tried to say something to comfort them both, but the words clogged in his throat. His mind felt torn by grief and pain. Memories of the last time he had seen his wife flooded his mind.

She'd come home and informed him that she was two months pregnant and he was the father. Except Seth knew that wasn't possible. In fact, he was almost positive he couldn't be little Miriam's *daed*. Because it had been a solid three months since he had seen Eve. Though he had claimed Miriam as his own for all outward appearances, it wasn't really true. At least, he didn't think so.

Even now as he looked at the fussy little girl, he could see no resemblance to him in her blue, almond-shaped eyes and rosebud lips. With her blond curls and rosy cheeks, she was the spitting image of Eve. Charming and pretty. With a loving disposition that made him want to protect them both. And he had failed miserably. Failed to get Eve off the drugs and failed to save her life.

Though Seth's name was on Miriam's birth certificate, he feared her biological father might one day come to claim the baby as his own. Seth had no idea who the man was or even if he knew he had a child. When Seth had asked Eve about it, she had insisted he was the father and that was the end of their discussions on the matter.

Regardless of the truth, Miriam was innocent of her creation. Eve's addictions weren't the baby's fault and Seth would never blame her. No matter what, Miriam was the child of his heart. He loved her more than anything and would do everything he could to protect her from the dark, horrible world Eve had become embroiled in.

Seth hadn't told his secret to anyone. Not even his kindly bishop, the leader of their *Gmay*, their Amish community there in Riverton. No one but him knew that Miriam was not his child. And he hoped Eve had taken the secret to her grave. Because once Seth said the words out loud, he could never take them back. And he would never take the chance of losing Miriam. Especially now that they had lost Eve.

"I'm so sorry, Seth. I don't know what to say, except I'm sorry and if there's anything I can do to help, I'll do it," Susanna said, her words filled with sympathy.

He nodded but still couldn't speak. The worst part about it was that he felt both sad and grateful at the same time. Eve had brought this on herself. She had been sick. He understood that. But she was also unwilling to get help. No amount of pleading from Seth or assistance from a counselor at the hospital in town had made a difference. She had lived a life that was eventually going to lead to this outcome. He just didn't think it would be this soon.

Now, a part of him wanted to cry and scream. Yet, another part was thankful it was finally over. No more uncertainty. No more wondering where his wife was, who she was with and what she was doing. No more surprises when she showed up in the middle of the night, yelling and screaming and carrying on until he was certain everyone in town could hear. No more embarrassment when he had to apologize to members of his *Gmay* because Eve had stolen drugs out of their medicine cabinets on church Sunday. No more fears that she might hurt Miriam when she wasn't in her right mind. And being relieved that Eve was gone made him feel guilty and ugly inside. Not like a man who loved *Gott* and cherished his wife and *familye*. And he realized he needed to heal from Eve's addictions, too. But poor Miriam. His little daughter would now grow up without a *mudder*.

Looking at Susanna, he wondered if she had felt the same when her Thomas died last year. She must have loved the man. At least Seth had Miriam, but Susanna now had no one. Just her elderly grandmother.

"I... I need to go to Pueblo," he murmured, as if to himself.

"*Ja*, of course you do. But a morgue is no place for a *boppli*. Can I look after Miriam for you while you are gone?" Susanna asked.

He caught the hesitant smile curving Susanna's pretty lips. An attractive woman in her own right, she was the complete opposite of Eve with reddish chestnut hair and amber-colored eyes. Susanna looked like a proper Amish woman, dressed in her simple black dress and white apron. Not a single strand of hair was out of place, so tidy beneath her starched, white prayer *kapp*. Her nose came to an impudent point at the end. No doubt she had a stubborn streak in her, just like Eve. But there was an inner strength and conviction in Susanna that was inspiring. And like him, Susanna had also lost her spouse. Seth knew her grandma had come to live with her shortly afterward, so she wouldn't be alone. But unlike him, Susanna would undoubtedly wed again. He would not. Because the trauma of being married to Eve had been enough to last him a lifetime. And no one must ever know the truth about Miriam.

He stood and glanced around the room, feeling out of sorts. "*Ja*, I'd appreciate it if you could take care of my *boppli* while I'm gone. I'll have to get a bus ticket or call Bob Crawley to drive me to Pueblo, if he's available. I have no idea when I'll be back."

Bob was an *Englisch* man whom the Amish frequently hired to drive them long distances in his car when it was too far for them to take their horses and buggies. But the man might not be available at this short notice. Depending on the bus schedule, it could be late evening before Seth returned home. He might even have to stay in Pueblo overnight and return sometime in the morning. One more delay to keep him from harvesting his potatoes. And without that crop, he could find himself in jeopardy of paying his mortgage.

"That sounds fine. I'll keep Miriam over at my place. *Mammi* and I will take *gut* care of her," Susanna said. "You might be gone until late. You can *komm* get her when you return. And I will send word to Bishop Yoder so he can assign some men to care for your livestock. You don't need to worry about a thing while you are gone."

Seth nodded, grateful for her insight. But it wasn't that simple. The men in his *Gmay* had their own farms to tend. He didn't expect them to dig his potatoes, too. Yet, it was the Amish way, to look after one another during times of trouble. Seth just wished Eve had been as thoughtful.

Susanna reached for a brown paper sack and started filling it with diapers, blankets and bottles for the baby. For good measure, she scooped up extra dirty clothing that was strewn across the floor and couch. He'd started sorting it but never got it laundered. Thankfully, he had found time to wash Miriam's diapers. He didn't question Susanna as he assisted, handing her any number of things Miriam might need while he was gone.

"*Danke.* I really appreciate your help," he said.

Susanna smiled but it didn't quite reach her amber eyes. For the first time since he'd known her, he thought she seemed sad, too. He wondered if she still missed her husband. And he envied the love and happiness they must have shared together. How he wished he and Eve could have had that kind of strong bond. He had tried but she'd let herself be controlled by substances she wasn't willing to let go of.

When he stepped near to kiss his daughter goodbye, Susanna's shoulders tensed, as if he made her nervous. He wasn't surprised. After all, up until a few minutes ago, he thought he was a married man. Someone from their *Gmay* could pass by the store and see her here with him. He didn't want to give anyone the wrong impression. It was best to send her on her way and avoid more gossip.

While Susanna carried Miriam downstairs, he packed the sack and walked with them outside into the chilled autumn air. It was a clear day, good for working in the fields. He felt morose and empty inside but there was work to be done. If his machinery and horses would cooperate, he could have his potatoes harvested within a few days. But first, he had to see about Eve.

Retrieving Miriam's riding safety chair, he placed it in Susanna's buggy. He helped her climb inside and watched as she strapped Miriam into her seat. Sensing that she was about to be parted from her daddy, the baby started to cry and reached for him. His heart melted.

"She'll be *allrecht*. I'll distract her," Susanna reassured him.

She soothed Miriam as she took the leather leads into her practiced grip and released the brake. As the buggy pulled away, Seth stepped back and waved goodbye. And for the first time, he wondered if it had been a coincidence that Susanna had been here right when he had needed her the most. When he'd received the worst news of his life, her compassion was touching and he knew Miriam was in good hands. But as they drove away and he walked toward the bus station, he realized he had never felt more alone in all his life.

Chapter Two

The following morning, Susanna sliced off several large chunks of dough and slapped each one onto the linen cheesecloth she'd laid across half of the kitchen table in her farmhouse. *Mammi* Dorothy, her grandmother, was using the other half of the table to chop vegetables for supper later that night. If Seth agreed to rent out his store to her, Susanna could move her noodle production over there. That would give them more room to cook meals.

Shaping each piece of dough into an elongated loaf, she breathed in the bland aroma of flour and raw eggs. Glancing over at Miriam, she smiled. The little girl sat in the high chair Susanna had hoped to one day use for her own children. The baby chortled happily as she shoved another chunk of scrambled egg into her mouth. Breakfast had consisted of oatmeal, eggs and fruit. Nutritious, fast, easy and filling. Using the meal as a diversion to both feed and entertain the child, Susanna had set Miriam in a corner of the cozy kitchen where she could keep an eye on her. Most of the meal had found its way into Miriam's mouth, but the girl was wearing a goodly portion on her face, arms and hands, too. As soon as the pasta was made and laid out in the drying racks, Susanna would clean up the baby.

The low growl of the gas-powered industrial-sized mixer filled the air. *Mammi* Dorothy stood over the machine, ensuring it blended the flour and eggs properly for another batch of dough. With long, cottony white hair combed back straight and tied in a bun beneath her prayer *kapp*, *Mammi* was still energetic and spry for her seventy-six years.

Glancing out the window, Susanna assessed Miriam's clothes, which she'd washed and hung on the line in the backyard the evening before. They should be almost dry now. She'd bring them in once the child went down for her morning nap. It seemed that, other than the baby's diapers, every piece of her clothing either smelled of sour milk or had stains on them. With Eve gone, Susanna figured Seth was struggling to keep up with his laundry. Even though it meant she went to bed late, Susanna had pulled out her old tub-style wringer washer and scrubbed each tiny article of clothing before hanging them up to dry through the night. Now, a coat of frost was on them but the warming sun would soon take care of that.

"We should go to Seth's apartment and gather up all his dirty clothes and give them a good wash, too," *Mammi* Dorothy spoke over the noise in the room.

Susanna nodded. "Maybe so. But that will have to wait for another day."

Mammi smiled, her gray eyes sparkling. She was a kindhearted woman and Susanna loved her dearly. Together, they made pasta two days each week, and Susanna enjoyed working with her grandmother. The farm Susanna's husband left her when he'd died wasn't large, only twenty acres. But now that she was a widow, Susanna was grateful to have a place of her own. She'd been more than happy when *Mammi* Dorothy came to live with her eleven months earlier.

At that moment, Miriam gave a squeal of delight and kicked her bare feet as she plunged another chunk of banana into her mouth.

The two women laughed.

"That *boppli* has a *gut* appetite and a sweet disposition. Any idea when Seth will *komm* pick her up?" *Mammi* asked with a chuckle.

"*Ne*, he wasn't sure how long his errand might take. I suspect he'll show up sometime this morning or afternoon at the latest," Susanna said.

She laid the roughly shaped loaves of dough on a large cookie sheet and carried them over to the roller. In the narrow workspace, she bumped against *Mammi's* shoulder.

"Excuse me," Susanna murmured, taking the opportunity to squeeze *Mammi's* arm.

Mammi smiled in response. Though the kitchen was large enough to accommodate a *familye* with a big table and chairs to seat eight, the industrial-sized pasta machine and drying racks took up lots of room and made it rather crowded. Which was one reason Susanna wanted to rent Seth's store. It'd be wonderful to move their business over to where they could sell more of their product. Currently, Susanna only sold locally to people she knew. But she really wanted to branch out so people on the street might pop in to buy her wares. She'd hoped to deal with this issue yesterday. But when Seth found out about his wife's death,

Susanna had watched his face drain of color. He must have been devastated by the news. No doubt he loved Eve very much. And a part of Susanna couldn't help feeling envious because her husband had never loved her. Not like that. Not even in the beginning, before he'd started drinking and lying about the house instead of doing his farm chores.

Since Thomas's death, Susanna had been struggling to repair her dilapidated home, barn and fences by herself. She didn't have the funds to hire the work done. Though she was determined, she wasn't as physically strong as a man. *Mammi* Dorothy was a big help but, between the noodles, fields and livestock they had to tend, they were busy and barely making ends meet. She had two acres planted in potatoes. Susanna hated to hire a man to plow and pick her spuds but didn't have much choice. She couldn't do it on her own but she needed the money badly. Financial security was slow going and Susanna wondered if her home would ever meet the high standards she'd been raised with. But there was little time to worry about that now. Determined to look at the bright side of life, she was grateful to have a roof over her head and the independence to do what she liked.

Lifting a loaf of dough, she fed it through the roller to flatten it out. Twice more, she pushed it through until it was nice and thin.

Yesterday wasn't the right time to press Seth about renting his store. Maybe later, when he'd had time to bury Eve. *Mammi* was more than willing to help Susanna look after Miriam. In fact, the baby's presence had brought laughter into their home, something Susanna had missed. When she was first married, she thought she'd be happy here. Thomas, her husband, had been so different during their short courtship. So kind, solicitous and considerate. But after their wedding, he'd changed overnight. And not for the better. Their short marriage had soured Susanna on the institution and she was happy to be done with it.

The rattle of a buggy outside drew Susanna's attention. Since her hands were dusted with flour, she used her elbow to part the plain curtains at the window. Morning sunlight gleamed across the yard as Seth's road horse pulled up in front of the farmhouse. He stepped out of the buggy, his face shadowed by his black felt hat.

"Seth's here now," Susanna said, speaking loud above the noise of the mixer.

Drawing away from the window, she wiped her hands on a cloth and glanced at *Mammi*.

Dorothy switched off the machine. "*Ach!* I thought he'd be a little bit later."

"Me, too. I'd better get the *boppli* bathed before she goes home with her *daed*. At least I can send her off clean and with a full tummy." Susanna looked at Miriam and released a low laugh.

The child literally had oatmeal and bananas from head to toe. The easiest way to tidy her up was with a full bath.

"*Ja*, you go do that while I bring in the laundry and offer Seth something to eat. I'll bet he's half-starved," Dorothy said.

"I'm sure he had something to eat during his travels," Susanna said, rubbing dough off her fingers.

Mammi Dorothy snorted with disgust. "Restaurant food. A man needs *gut* home cooking to fill him up, not that prepackaged stuff."

As Susanna covered the loaves of dough so they wouldn't dry out, she hid a silent laugh. *Mammi's* solution to all problems was to feed everyone a hearty, home-cooked meal. And it usually worked, too. After all, it was difficult to stay down in the dumps while eating one of *Mammi's* homemade cinnamon rolls frosted with powdered sugar icing.

As Susanna picked up Miriam and carried her toward the doorway, Dorothy placed a frying pan on the stovetop. When Susanna returned with the baby twenty minutes later, the clothes had been brought in from the line and Seth sat at the kitchen table, eating scrambled eggs, crispy bacon and thick slices of fresh bread spread with homemade peach jam. For dessert, an enormous cinnamon roll sat on a plate beside his glass of milk.

"Guder mariye," Susanna spoke low.

"Hallo," Seth returned, coming immediately to his feet.

Susanna blinked in surprise and stepped over to the sink. Wow! Thomas had never stood for her when she walked into the room.

As his gaze swept over Miriam, Seth's eyes looked tired, bloodshot and careworn. Susanna doubted he'd slept the night before. The Amish tried not to show outward signs of grief, relying on *Gott's* will instead. But losing his wife so young couldn't be easy for Seth. As Miriam grew up, it wouldn't be easy for her, either.

Upon seeing her dad, the baby chortled gleefully and held out her arms to him. Seth reached over and took her before kissing her forehead. From the look of adoration in his eyes, Susanna had no doubt he loved his child.

"Hmm. She smells *gut*," he remarked as he cuddled the baby close.

Susanna nodded, stepping away from him. "That's the baby lotion I used. She just had a bath. You should have seen her after her breakfast. She was wearing more food than she ate."

A low chuckle rumbled in his chest and he kissed the baby again, then closed his eyes for several long seconds, as if he were breathing her in. Finally, he sat down and placed the girl on his knee, holding her with one large hand while he picked up his fork and resumed eating his meal.

"How did it go in Pueblo?" Susanna asked as she lifted the tray to the high chair and took it over to the sink for a good washing.

She glanced over her shoulder at him. Holding a spatula aloft in the air, *Mammi* paused a moment to gaze at Seth, too. Her expression was filled with kind sympathy as she awaited his response.

Seth ducked his head over his plate and released a heavy sigh. "As well as can be expected. I had to identify the body."

"It was definitely Eve, then?" *Mammi* asked.

Seth nodded and stared thoughtfully at his daughter, his voice quiet and introspective. "*Ja*, it was my wife."

"*Ach*, I'm so sorry, Seth. It's such an awful thing to happen to someone so young. It's such a waste," *Mammi* said.

"*Ja*, such a waste," Seth echoed in a soft voice that Susanna almost didn't hear.

"Do you know when the funeral will take place?" she asked.

Seth set his fork down and shook his head. "*Ne*, not until the medical examiner releases her body. I should hear some news in the next week or so. Then, I can make more definite plans for her burial."

Susanna rinsed and dried the tray to the high chair, thinking. Though Eve had been shunned by their people, she was dead and they would see to her funeral, because Seth and Miriam were still in good standing with their *Gmay* and needed compassion right now. Susanna longed to help Seth somehow but her common sense told her she had enough troubles of her own. She didn't want to get mixed up with this problem. And yet, she felt empathy for him and his motherless baby.

"Was Eve definitely alone when she died? There was no foul play?" Susanna asked.

He looked up, his forehead crinkled with consternation. Then, he shrugged. "There's no way to know. The police said her body was found in a park in Pueblo. She still had her purse with her and there was money in it, so she hadn't been robbed. That's how they knew where to find me. The police identified her from her library card, which included our home address. I suspect we'll never know exactly what happened the night she died."

"I see. I'm so glad she didn't end up being a Jane Doe," Susanna said. "I'm guessing you'll want to talk to Bishop Yoder. I went to see him yesterday, to tell him what happened. He said he was going to send several men over to your place in the afternoon to care for your livestock while you were gone."

Seth met her gaze, his eyes filled with angst. "*Ja*, they did more than that. They started plowing and gathering my potatoes. I saw their work when I arrived *heemet* early this morning. They have half my field picked. I didn't expect so much generosity. Everyone's been very kind."

Susanna nodded. "It's the least we can do. The men will be over to your place later this morning to finish your harvest. You've got enough on your mind without worrying about your potatoes, too."

Mammi patted Seth's arm. "I just wish we could do more."

Seth showed a wan smile as he scooted back his chair. "*Ach*, I best get *heemet* now. I don't want the men to arrive while I'm not there to help with the work."

Susanna glanced at his plate. "But you haven't finished your breakfast."

"I… I'm afraid I don't have much of an appetite. But it was delicious." He smiled his thanks at *Mammi*, then stood, holding Miriam close beneath his chin.

Without being asked, *Mammi* placed his cinnamon roll in a plastic container with a lid and handed it to him. "You can eat this later."

"*Danke,*" he said.

"Why don't you leave the *boppli* here with *Mammi* and me for the day? We can look after her while you work."

The moment she said the words, Susanna regretted her offer. She didn't have time to tend someone else's child. The last thing she wanted was to become attached to a cute baby and her heartbroken father. But how could Susanna refuse? After all, Seth's needs were great right now. This was an act of service and what the Lord would want her to do.

"Later this afternoon, I'll be taking a new quilt I just finished over to the general store to sell on consignment. I could bring Miriam *heemet* to you on my way back," *Mammi* said.

Seth blinked. "That would be so helpful. Are you sure it's not too much of an imposition?"

Mammi waved a hand in the air before reaching to take Miriam from him. "Of course not. Miriam's a sweet, easygoing *boppli*. She hardly frets at all. You'll need something to eat, too. I'll put a loaf of homemade bread and soup in your fridge for your supper later tonight. You'll just need to warm it up."

"*Danke*. Miriam's been sweet from the beginning. She's easy to love. I'm blessed to have her in my life," Seth said.

His words caused a lump to rise in Susanna's chest. How she wished she'd been able to have a child before Thomas died but he hadn't given her even that.

Seth stepped over to the door and she followed him out. Standing on the back porch, she took a deep inhale of brisk, morning air before letting it go. Her heart reached out to Miriam. Susanna's own mother had died before she was two years old, shortly after her father abandoned them. Susanna had been raised by her grandparents. Like Susanna, Miriam would now grow up always wondering what her *mamm* was like and if her life might have been happier if her mother had been there.

Looking after Miriam was the least Susanna could do. But as soon as Seth got his feet beneath him, that would have to end. Because Susanna had a business and farm to run. She didn't have time to worry about Seth's cute baby girl. And that was that.

Seth stepped out onto Susanna's back porch. The screen door clapped closed behind him. Glancing at the sullen sky, he saw that it was filled with scattered clouds. Perfect fall weather for plowing up potatoes. But he knew the heavens could open up and spill rain or snow any day now. He needed to get his spuds harvested. Fast.

"Are you sure you and your *grossmudder* don't mind looking after Miriam for another day?" Seth asked.

He didn't look at Susanna but felt her curiosity as she stood apart from him. Though they'd offered to watch Miriam for him, he felt like he was imposing heavily on them. After all, Susanna had her own farm to tend. A quick glance at her fields told him she hadn't harvested her potatoes, either. Without a husband to help her, Susanna might let Seth return her kindness by doing that for her over the next few days. Since the men of his congregation had helped him so much, he now had time to return the favor for Susanna.

"Of course not. *Mammi* and I know you're in a bit of a bind right now. *Mammi* will bring Miriam to you later, after your work is done," Susanna said.

Though her words sounded genuine, he caught a hint of hesitancy in her voice as she stepped away from him. Hopefully, she really meant what she said.

He glanced at the large red barn and saw the peeling paint and wide double doors hanging crooked on their hinges. Likewise, the fence rails surrounding the corrals sat twisted and rickety. It wouldn't take much for her cows to knock them down. She definitely needed help and he made a mental note to do what he could to set these things right for her.

"I'm glad the police were able to find you.

Now you can bring Eve *heemet* where she belongs," Susanna said.

Seth nodded. "When I saw her last night, her body looked so thin. Like she hadn't been eating much."

Susanna blinked and made a sad little sound in the back of her throat. Seth realized maybe he should not have told her that but the words just poured out of his mouth.

"Why do you think that is?" Susanna asked.

Seth shrugged. "The coroner told me that drug addicts often forget to eat. All they can think about is getting their next fix. They don't think about nourishment or…anything else."

Okay, he was definitely telling her too much. And though Susanna seemed uneasy around him, she was much too easy to talk to for some odd reason.

She drew in a quick breath. "I can't imagine that, but I don't know much about drug addiction."

He smiled, feeling wretched inside. "That's a *gut* thing. I'm glad you're innocent to such worldly ways, Susanna. I wish Eve had been more like you."

She tilted her head and gazed at him, her eyes filled with confusion and shock. "Like me?"

"*Ja*, you're always busy working. I know

you have goals and things you want to accomplish in life. I wish Eve had been industrious like you. Maybe if she'd had some aspirations and kept busy doing *gut* activities, she'd still be safe at *heemet*, where she belongs."

They didn't speak for a few moments and the autumn breeze ruffled the golden leaves of the cottonwood tree overhead. More leaves of red, brown and yellow scattered across the narrow road leading to her front yard.

"Seth, I know this is hard on you and Miriam, but please believe me when I say it'll get easier," Susanna said.

"Have things gotten easier for you now that some time has passed since Thomas died?" he asked.

Seth had known her husband briefly. Thomas hadn't been a friendly man. In fact, just the opposite. He'd been rather grim and surly with everyone in their congregation. Once, Seth had even witnessed Thomas yelling and gripping Susanna's arm in anger. And during the barn raisings and other community work projects they'd helped with, Thomas did more sitting than labor. From the shabby condition of his farm, Thomas hadn't been much for hard work. Which didn't sit well with the Amish, who had a work ethic second to none.

But since Susanna hadn't remarried, Seth figured she must still miss her husband a lot.

She nodded. "*Ja*, it's much easier now. Just don't lose your faith in the Lord. Faith has brought me a lot of strength during difficult times in my life. I know it can help you, too. Trust in *Gott*."

For the first time since he'd met her, Seth looked at Susanna. Really looked at her. And all of a sudden, he saw a beautiful, good woman who was just as grief-stricken as him. Someone who understood what it was like to lose their spouse, along with all their wishes and dreams. But unlike him, Seth hoped Susanna never knew the angst of betrayal. Though he would never say so, he knew Eve had cheated on him. She'd thrown it in his face numerous times. That's why she'd finally been shunned for adultery. He just hoped people in his *Gmay* didn't put it together and suspect that Miriam wasn't his child. A part of him thought Eve had gotten what she deserved. Another part had compassion for the ugly life she'd been leading. He knew angry thoughts were uncharitable, unkind and selfish. And yet, he couldn't seem to help it.

He nodded at his horse. "*Ach*, I'd best get going."

Susanna nodded and folded her arms against the sharp breeze as she walked toward the door. It was almost as if she were eager for him to leave.

Seth stepped off the porch and forced himself to get into his buggy. The last thing he wanted to do right now was work in his fields. His brain felt out of sorts and fogged by grief. He'd rather stay here at Susanna's farm, with Miriam. But work would help take his mind off his troubles. It would also ensure he could pay his bills and put food on the table.

Susanna went inside and Seth slapped the leather leads against the horse's rump. It took only a few minutes to drive a mile down the road to his own farm. As he passed through town, he thought about how Susanna and *Mammi* Dorothy had been so welcoming. So kind and understanding of his predicament. As he'd sat in their cozy kitchen and eaten a meal, he'd felt the warmth of *familye* surrounding him…a feeling he hadn't enjoyed since he was a teenaged boy. Then, Susanna had brought Miriam to him. The baby had been so cheerful and smelled so clean, just like a baby should. He could tell she'd received the best of care in their home. Dorothy's offer to look after the girl was a huge blessing in his life right now. He hated leaving Miriam but there was work to be done. Though he wasn't thinking clearly, there was no time to grieve now. It was harvest season and he needed his potato crop gathered in so he could provide for his daughter.

Correction. Eve's daughter.

He thought about his trip to the hospital in Pueblo to identify Eve's body. Lying on a cold slab, she'd had dark circles beneath her eyes from harsh living and her face had looked so pale and gaunt. Covered by a white sheet, she'd appeared so quiet and still. Like she was finally at peace. Though she'd never loved him the way he'd tried to love her, Eve was his wife and Miriam's mother. Now, she was gone. And after he'd returned home early that morning, he'd sat inside his apartment alone and wept over her loss. And he vowed then that he'd never cry over another woman again.

If Susanna hadn't been there for him, he didn't know what he would have done. Dragging Miriam with him to the morgue in Pueblo would have been traumatic for both of them. Now, he had to keep going. Had to focus on Miriam and his work.

Later, once his potatoes were harvested, Dorothy would bring Miriam over to his place.

And for some odd reason, Seth anticipated the visit. He just wished it was Susanna who was bringing Miriam home. As a married man, he'd never even looked at another woman. But now, he found something about Susanna quite remarkable. Something he didn't understand or even want to contemplate. Because, no matter what, he was never going to marry again. He would not allow Miriam to become a casualty of Eve's reckless life. The child must be his first priority. Not the pretty widow who was helping him look after his little daughter.

Chapter Three

"The funeral will be held this next Saturday."

Holding her fork in one hand, Susanna looked up from her plate of food and gazed at Sarah Yoder, the bishop's wife. The woman stood a few feet away, her expression one of sympathy and support.

Sitting at a long table inside the bishop's spacious barn, Susanna was having lunch with the other women of her congregation. It was church Sunday. Having completed their meetings earlier that morning, they'd just finished feeding the men and children, who were now outside in the yard playing and visiting. The day was cool and gray. Soon, the cold weather would drive them inside.

Light glimmered on dust motes filtering through the open doorway. A fragrant breeze rustled through the tall rafters overhead. Leaves of orange and brown scattered across the ground. If they weren't planning a funeral, it would be a normal, fall day.

"How did it happen? How did Eve die?" Abby Fisher asked, her eyes crinkled with sadness.

"It was a drug overdose," old Marva Geingerich hissed. As the stern matriarch of their congregation, she frequently made her disapproval known to all.

"And they found her in Pueblo?" Linda Hostetler asked in a gentle and concerned voice.

Marva nodded, pursing her lips together. "That's what they said. She was living with *Englisch* men who weren't her husband. Just shameful."

The room erupted into a barrage of titters as the women discussed Eve's shocking behavior.

Tessa Yoder spoke what was on Susanna's mind. "Poor Seth and Miriam. Seth must be heartbroken."

Sitting beside Susanna, *Mammi* Dorothy leaned forward and fixed her gaze on the group of women. "*Ja*, I'm sure he is. That's why we should focus on what we can do to help. After all, Seth is one of our own."

Sarah Yoder opened her mouth to speak, but Norma Albrecht cut her off.

"But why didn't Eve *komm* home? She could have repented and changed her ways. We would have taken care of her. What was she doing in Pueblo?"

"She ran off after she was shunned. She was doing drugs and living with strange men. Seth couldn't take her body away from the morgue until the medical examiner got a bunch of toxic tests back," Mary Schwartz said.

"Toxicology test results," Susanna corrected the woman.

"That's right. And once they knew the cause of death, they released Eve's body so Seth can bury her. The poor man. It's already been three weeks since she died," Henrietta Burkholder said.

Linda Hostetler's eyes rounded in surprise. "What did the police say about it?"

Marva pointed a bony finger at Susanna. "Ask her. I heard she was there when they came to tell Seth that Eve had died."

Susanna blinked in surprise, feeling suddenly attacked and wishing she could fade into the floor. Most of the women were saddened to hear about Eve's death. They adhered to Jesus Christ's teachings to love one another and leave the judgment to *Gott*. But like some people in any religion, a few women seemed only interested in the juicy tidbits of information. Having been the brunt of painful gossip before, the last thing Susanna wanted was to participate in more of the same. Instead, she stared at the ham, pickles and a thick slice of homemade bread smeared with peanut butter that rested on her plate. Suddenly, she'd lost her appetite. There was no way she was going to confide the few things she knew about Eve's demise. Out of respect for Seth and Miriam, she couldn't do that. It wouldn't be kind and it definitely wasn't necessary.

The room went quiet as everyone waited with bated breath to hear what she might say. Finally, she spoke in a soft, nonconfrontational voice.

"All I know is that Seth has lost his wife and Miriam has lost her *mudder*. I don't think any of this hearsay is pertinent to what we're planning to feed people at the funeral. Let's focus on helping Seth and Miriam and remember that we've lost one of our own. The *familye* is still grieving Eve's loss. We must have compassion for them."

"Well said," Sarah Yoder interjected with a firm nod. "We'll need to feed approximately one hundred and fifty people. Let's focus on that."

As they made plans to provide sliced hams, potato casseroles, dinner rolls and a variety of salads and pies, Susanna breathed a sigh of relief. She was grateful to get the attention off her and back on the matter at hand. But soon, the discussion turned back to rumors about Eve and her wild ways. When *Mammi* Dorothy gasped suddenly, Susanna looked up.

Seth stood in the open doorway, holding Miriam in his arms. His overly long hair looked clean and slicked back out of his eyes. He wore his best Sunday jacket. From his dark expression, Susanna knew he'd overheard at least part of their dialogue. Even little Miriam looked sober with displeasure, gazing at the crowd of women with her bright blue eyes. And Susanna was beyond grateful that she'd refused to participate in any scandalous chatter. For some odd reason, it was more than important to her that she not add any extra pain to Seth's already shattered heart.

Everyone went absolutely still. An uncomfortable silence clung to the air. Looking rather startled, Sarah Yoder walked over to the doorway and lifted a hand to rest on Seth's shoulder.

"Seth, we're just planning what to serve at the funeral luncheon. What can we do for you?" Sarah asked kindly.

His gaze lifted to rest on Susanna and his eyes were unblinking. "I'd like to speak with Susanna in private for a few minutes, please."

Susanna swallowed hard and her heart felt like it sank down to her feet. *Mammi* rested a hand on her arm, as if to offer her steady support.

"*Ja*, of course," Susanna said.

Standing, she leaned against her grandmother as she lifted one leg over the bench seat, then the other, before joining Seth at the door. As she left the barn, she heard several whispers behind her and knew she'd just become the topic of conversation. She hoped the women's words were nice and helpful, not cruel and biting. No doubt, *Mammi* would fill her in on what transpired once they returned home and were alone later that evening.

Outside in the yard, a frigid breeze rustled the barren tree limbs overhead. Seth stepped away from the crowd of men who stood conversing on the yellowed lawn. Children skirted past them in a game of chase. In an open field, the teenaged kids had started playing baseball. Everyone was enjoying the last of the good weather before winter hit. Things seemed normal and happy. Except they weren't. Not for Seth.

He walked over to where two vacant chairs rested beneath the long barren branches of an elm tree and indicated that Susanna should sit down. The wind whipped the ties to her prayer *kapp* around her shoulders and she pulled them back into place. Thankfully, little Miriam was dressed warm with a gray knit cap pulled over her ears.

"*Ne, danke.* I'd rather stand," Susanna said.

She twined her hands together, feeling nervous and a bit grouchy by all that had transpired.

"What is it you want?" she asked, ignoring Miriam when the baby reached for her. Instead, Susanna forced herself to meet Seth's gaze.

"I just spoke to Bishop Yoder at length about everything going on in my life," he said.

Susanna frowned and mentally shook her head. She knew this was a difficult time for Seth but couldn't see what that had to do with her.

"And?" she pressed.

"And I'd like to make a deal with you."

Her attention perked up.

"Go on," she said, feeling uneasy and trying to still the pattering of her rapid pulse.

"I would like to rent out my store to you in exchange for you providing childcare for Miriam," he said.

Susanna's heart sank. She couldn't believe she had heard him correctly. She definitely wanted to rent out his store. But tend the baby on a regular basis? That was not part of her plans.

"You want to rent your store to me but you also want me to watch Miriam for you?" she restated his words, trying to grasp their meaning and how such an arrangement would ever work in her daily life.

"That's correct. No one else lives as close to my farm as you do. Your place is nearby, so it'll be easy for me to get Miriam over to you rather than driving her out to one of the other women at their farms. I won't charge you any money to rent the store. My payment would be the childcare you would provide. I know you'll be busy but I hoped you might be amenable to my proposal," he said.

She opened her mouth to refuse but he didn't give her the opportunity.

"My apartment is right upstairs," he hurried on. "That's handy because all of Miriam's things would be close by. During nap times, you could keep working while you listen for her, in case she wakes up. But I have to go outside and work in the barn and fields. Can't we make this work somehow? Please, Susanna?"

The way he said her name and the quiet pleading in his voice did something to her inside. It was a cry for help. Almost begging. He sounded earnest and...

Desperate.

"I don't know if it will work, Seth. I've got my own farm to tend, too. I need to hire some men to plow and pick my potatoes this week, or I will lose the crop," she said, speaking the honest truth.

"I will take care of that for you...for free. There! You no longer have to worry about it," he said.

Hmm. That alone made his offer really tempting. But what if she didn't hear Miriam wake up? What if she had customers but had to dash upstairs to get the baby, first? What if she was running noisy mixers and didn't know the child was crying? And how could she get everything done efficiently? She didn't want to wear out *Mammi* with an increased workload, either. Even if Seth harvested her potatoes, there weren't enough hours in the day to do all her farm chores and also make the noodle store prosperous while tending a tiny baby, too. Was there?

"Thanks to the men in our *Gmay*, my potatoes have been harvested. I'll bring my potato digger over to your place first thing tomorrow morning. I'll also do some repair work on your barn and fences. I figure we can team up to get the work done."

Susanna's mouth dropped open in surprise. He'd really thought this through, hadn't he? With his forty and her twenty acres, he'd be one busy farmer. But she'd be busy, too.

"I think we can help each other out, Susanna. I need you and you need me. Can't we give it a try? Please?" he asked.

No! No! She didn't want to need any man. Not ever again.

"You… You're planning to harvest for me?" she said, trying to be practical. Trying to give in to common sense. But her fear of losing her independence was not easy to push aside. Still, his offer was a good one. With his help, she wouldn't need to hire someone else to harvest her potatoes. And she'd be able to stash the extra cash for other needs.

The color of his hazel eyes deepened to a brilliant green. "*Ja*, I figure I can get your potatoes dug up and picked within a couple of days. If we work together, there is no reason we can't both have a prosperous harvest."

Oh, that sounded so wonderful. Not once since she had married Thomas had her farm produced a bountiful crop. At first, she thought it was because their farm had poor soil. But that didn't make sense. The dirt in her fields looked as dark and rich with nutrients as everyone else's in the area. And the vegetable garden she tended on her own had produced well. After two years, she'd finally arrived at the realization that she was spread too thin and just couldn't tend her crops effectively without Thomas's help. As a result, she never gleaned a nice harvest and barely made ends meet.

In contrast, Seth's fields always burgeoned with life. In years past, she'd seen him out working from sunup to sundown. Dedicated and untiring. If he helped her, she would undoubtedly have enough funds to pay her bills and put a little aside for a rainy day. If all went well, perhaps she could afford to buy a bigger dough mixer, too.

"*Allrecht*. Let's give it a try. But in the meantime, I would appreciate it if you would continue looking for more suitable childcare elsewhere. Perhaps one of the older girls or another woman in our *Gmay* might be willing to watch Miriam for you. She is a sweet *boppli*, after all."

But even as she said the words, Susanna didn't like the thought of Miriam going to someone else. And that didn't make sense. Miriam wasn't her baby. It shouldn't matter to Susanna where the little girl went, but it did.

Seth exhaled a sigh of relief. "I promise to do that. But I have already asked around many times and no one seems interested in permanent childcare for my *dochder*. They are willing to help temporarily, but transportation is a problem. Most of our people live far outside of town. They can't spend the day sitting around at my place and it's difficult for me to take the time to drive Miriam over to their farms and pick her up each evening. I would be on the road for hours every day. With winter coming on, that's not *gut* for the *boppli*."

Susanna nodded in understanding. Back

east, the Amish farms were close together. But this was Colorado, where the farms were miles and miles apart. And even if an older teenaged girl was willing to go to Seth's home, she'd still have to drive to and from his place every day. That could suck up a great deal of time and prove a hardship once snow started falling. In the outlying areas, the drifts came awful deep. It would not be good for a young girl to be stranded along the road somewhere all alone. But Susanna lived close by. She was the obvious best choice…if she could make it work.

She glanced at Miriam and smiled. The baby had laid her cheek against her daddy's chest and was sucking her thumb contentedly as she gazed quietly at Susanna with those big, shining blue eyes of hers. And once more, the thought of sending this little girl off to someone else filled Susanna with misgivings and doubt. But then, she hardened her will. This was not her child. She had her ambitions and needed to put herself and *Mammi* first. And no widowed man and his sweet little daughter were going to worm their way into her heart.

Seth couldn't believe Susanna had agreed to his proposition. She was willing to look after Miriam…for the time being. And he was even pleased that the store would finally be packed with merchandise and open for business. But what if things didn't work out? He had just spent the last half hour discussing his options with Bishop Yoder. Seth could sell the store and his farm and make a tidy return on his investment. He could pack up Miriam and relocate to Indiana, where he had *familye* who would help him raise his daughter. And one day, he might even be able to afford to buy his own farm again, but he doubted it. Land was much more expensive back east. In the meantime, his older brother was fairly established and would let Seth work for him. Miriam could grow up with her cousins and be happy. And Seth would grow old with no wife or place to call his own.

"Just one more thing," Susanna said.

His senses went on high alert. "And what is that?"

"If, after Christmas, our arrangement is not working out for either of us, we will end it and go our separate ways. Does that agree with you?" she asked.

Seth nodded and looked away. A sense of foreboding pulsed over him. Selling the store would break his heart. Mostly because it would be the ultimate failure. That building was a symbol of a better time when he still had hope that he and Eve could be happy together. But now, he had already been unsuccessful in saving his wife. He couldn't fail at his farm, too. He was determined to keep it, if for no other reason than the fact that he did not want to return to Indiana. He wanted to raise his daughter here in Colorado, where she could grow up knowing her father had a prosperous farm and that he had fought to keep it for her.

"*Ja*, that agrees with me. But Susanna... I'm determined to make this work, no matter what. I hope you are, too," he said.

Her eyes widened and she pursed her lips together, not in disapproval, but in a look of resolution.

"*Ja*, I... I am. I think we are both goal oriented. Neither of us wants to give up on our dreams," she said.

Wow! She really did understand him after all. And for the first time in his life, he thought he'd finally met another person who was as willful, hardworking and ambitious as him.

"That's right," he said.

"Then, we have this figured out?" she asked.

He nodded, filled with a new appreciation for the arrangement they had just agreed upon. "*Ja*, I think we understand each other perfectly."

"*Gut!* The week after the funeral, *Mammi* and I will *komm* over to the store first thing to tend Miriam…just as soon as I've fed my livestock. I'd like to start setting out my merchandise immediately. It shouldn't take long before I can open up for business. I can start looking after Miriam as soon as I arrive. If I have to travel back to my place to retrieve loads of boxes, I will just take Miriam with me or leave *Mammi* at the store to tend her," she said.

"That sounds fine. Whatever works for you. And I wanted to say *danke* to you."

"For what?" she asked.

"For refusing to give the gossips more fodder about Eve and me," he said.

Her mouth dropped open. "You overheard what was being said in the barn?"

He nodded. "I did. Most of it, I think. And I appreciate your words of support."

She tugged her woolen cloak tighter together at her throat, then rested her hand against her waist. He almost smiled at the impudent way she lifted her chin higher in the air.

"Most of those women mean well and have nothing but compassion for what you and Miriam are going through," she said. "But some of them need to be taught a lesson by the Savior's commandment to love one another."

Ducking his head, he silently agreed as he gave his daughter a happy squeeze. The baby smiled and chortled something only she could comprehend. She lifted a little hand toward the bishop's farmhouse and pointed, chattering in her nonsensical speech.

"It looks like Miriam approves of our agreement, too," he said.

Susanna laughed, the sound high and sweet. A sound he'd rarely heard from Eve. It caused something to soften inside him. An emotion he didn't understand.

"*Ja*, she's such an agreeable *boppli. Mammi* loves her and I'm sure we will get along fine together," Susanna said.

She glanced at him and her smile faded, as if she didn't like sharing this cheerful moment with him.

She looked away. The women were coming out of the barn. Some were carrying empty serving bowls and platters, indicating they had finished lunch and were ready to start clearing away the meal before going home.

"*Ach*, I guess I better go help. I don't want *Mammi* to overdo with the cleanup," Susanna said, stepping toward the barn.

"*Ja*, I'll be over tomorrow, to harvest your potatoes," he said, unable to deny a euphoric feeling of victory as it swelled inside his chest.

Finally, he had arranged for quality child-care for Miriam. He could now work in the barn and fields without fear. He was determined to make his and Susanna's farms prosper. Hopefully, Susanna would be so pleased with the results that she'd continue to use his store and look after Miriam for several years to come.

"*Mach's gut*," Susanna said, before turning and walking away.

"Goodbye," he returned.

Watching her go, Seth noticed several of the women were looking at him with pity in their eyes. They ducked their heads close and whispered together and he could just imagine what they were saying. None of them understood about Eve. Not really. And he couldn't blame them. Even he could not grasp what had possessed his wife to do the things she'd done. Her addictions and worldly ways were alien to them all. Something they shunned and could not comprehend. It just wasn't part of their thoughts or everyday existence.

Her funeral would take place in a few days' time. Then, the rumors would die down and Seth could resume a normal life, raising his daughter to the best of his ability. With Susanna and her grandma Dorothy's help, he could ensure Miriam received quality care… at least until Christmastime. But a bit of doubt nibbled at his mind. What if Susanna didn't like the arrangement? What if Miriam was too much trouble? Seth silently prayed everything worked out fine and they could make this a permanent plan.

He shook his head, forcing the uncertainty from his thoughts. Over the past few years, he had learned to take things one day at a time and live by faith. And right now, that was all he dared hope for.

Chapter Four

An array of dark umbrellas shielded Eve's gravesite from the drizzling rain. Sitting adjacent to Bishop Yoder's north pasture, the Amish cemetery nestled smack dab in the middle of his farmland, sectioned off by nothing more than a white rail fence. The bleak sky and heavy chill in the air suited the somber fall day perfectly. Black buggies and horses lined the outer perimeter of the graveyard. Over a hundred Amish men, women and children crowded around the mound of dirt and gaping hole where Eve Lehman would finally be laid to rest.

Simple and distinctive, the gray granite headstone was already in place and bore Eve's full name, birth and death dates, her age in years, months and days, and the Germanic words *Finde frieden im Himmel*.

Find peace in Heaven.

Gazing at the stone, Susanna thought it was an appropriate sentiment. Huddled beside *Mammi*, she lifted her gaze to where Seth stood beside Bishop Yoder and Deacon Albrecht at the top of the burial site. Following a short sermon, they'd had a prayer and sang a farewell hymn called *"Lebt Friedsam."* The haunting Germanic words lifted over the vast valley and craggy Wet Mountains to the east. Susanna wasn't surprised by the inscription Seth had included on his wife's stone. Everyone knew Eve had been a troubled person. But now, Eve was in *Gott*'s care and Susanna was worried about Seth. He had a lot on his plate with a farm and baby to raise by himself.

Hunching his broad shoulders against the frigid breeze, he pulled the brim of his black felt hat down low so that it shadowed his eyes. His blunt jaw was locked hard as marble. With one arm, he cradled little Miriam close against his chest, shielding her from the elements. In his right hand, he held a black umbrella, his knuckles white from such a strong grip. Dressed warm and wrapped in a heavy blanket, the baby tucked her face beneath her *daed*'s chin and sucked her thumb, completely oblivious that she'd lost her *mudder*. Susanna wasn't certain, but sometime during the sermon, she thought the child had fallen asleep, sheltered in her father's arms. In spite of Seth's strength, the two of them looked so sad and lonely standing there.

So vulnerable.

As the men lowered the simple pine box into the ground, Seth looked up and Susanna saw the pain in his expressive eyes. Maybe he wasn't as strong as she thought. Maybe...

"We bid farewell to our sister Eve. Now, let us return to my home where we invite all of you to share a simple meal together," Bishop Yoder spoke to the crowd.

The gathering horde seemed to breathe a collective sigh of finality as they disbanded. Almost everyone headed for their buggies, some hanging back with their umbrellas to visit together for a few minutes. Susanna knew they would all return to the bishop's large barn, where they would enjoy their meal. All the women had helped with the preparations, including Susanna and *Mammi*. Then, everyone would go home and Seth and Miriam would return to their regular activities, barely missing a beat. For the Amish, death was a part of life. They accepted it as

Gott's will. But the fact that Eve had died so young was such a shame.

"*Ach*, that's it, then," *Mammi* said, glancing at Seth. "He is a widower and his *boppli* is an orphan. The poor dears. Brr! It's too cold to stand here any longer. I will wait for you in the buggy."

Susanna nodded. "*Ja*, you go get warm, *Mammi*. I will be along shortly."

She watched as her grandmother stepped over to the dirt path, skirting puddles as she went, and joined several other women as they made their way outside the white fence. Susanna planned to return to the bishop's house and help set out the noon meal, but something held her back. Seth looked up and caught her eye, holding her there. She wanted to move away. To follow her grandmother to the buggy. But it felt as though her feet were nailed to the ground. She wanted to say something consoling to Seth but didn't know what. No words could bring him solace. Only his faith and the Savior's love could do that.

Five strong men from her congregation picked up shovels and started to fill in the grave. Dressed all in black, they didn't speak as they worked in quiet companionship, tossing damp dirt over the coffin in rapid succession.

Seth stood gazing at her, solemn and un-movable. Then, he stepped over to her and gave a curt nod of his head.

"Susanna."

"Seth."

She felt awkward and out of place. Over the past few days, he had kept his word and harvested her potatoes and arranged for a buyer. Knowing her spuds were safely out of the ground and sold brought her a great deal of peace. For that act alone, she owed Seth a lot. But even so, she didn't like being this close to him.

"I'm so sorry for your loss," she said.

He nodded, tucking the blankets tighter around Miriam. "*Danke.* I appreciate that."

"I am sure Eve is finally at peace."

He blinked and glanced at the headstone. "I hope so."

"How are you holding up?" Susanna asked, wondering what else she could say to ease his grief.

"As well as can be expected." His words sounded muffled and without enthusiasm.

"And how is Miriam doing?" She smiled and reached out to take hold of the baby's fingers where they peeked out from beneath folds of the quilt.

He shrugged one shoulder. "She is not quite ten months old. Right now, she has no idea what has happened. But later when she's older, she'll miss her *mudder* terribly, I think."

"You could make a list of good memories of her *mamm*, to tell Miriam about when she's old enough to understand," Susanna suggested.

His eyes flickered with uncertainty. "That's a *gut* idea, but I'm afraid it may be a rather short list."

How sad! Susanna's heart went out to him. But then, she stopped herself. After all, she didn't know this man well. Not really. He was nothing to her except her brother in Jesus Christ. And yet, she felt drawn to him. Maybe because she had been there when the police brought him the news of Eve's death. And also because Susanna was a widow, too. Whatever the reason, she was determined to squelch it now. She had plans that did not include a man in her life. She couldn't allow herself to become embroiled in Seth's affairs.

"*Ach*, I guess I had best be going now," she said.

He lifted his face into the wind and took a deep, cleansing breath before releasing it. "*Ja*, you should return to the house and get out of this cold air."

She took a step back, feeling a bit jittery. As if there was something more to say.

"*Mammi* has just returned to the buggy. The weather is ugly but the sermon was quite nice," she said.

"*Ja*, the weather is fitting for the day. It's going to get colder, too."

He peered at her with bloodshot eyes and she thought he must have had a sleepless night.

Two women and men headed toward their buggies, tossing knowing smiles in their direction. Susanna shifted her weight nervously, knowing what they were thinking. Both she and Seth had lost their spouses. Seth had a young child to raise and needed to remarry as soon as possible. No doubt, Susanna was their chosen target. She could just imagine their wagging tongues later at the luncheon as everyone in her congregation paired her with Seth. But she was going to have to disappoint them all because it was not going to happen.

"Goodbye," she said and turned.

"Wait! Would… Would you be willing to take Miriam back to the bishop's house and look after her for me a little while? I… I would like to help fill in the grave and the cold isn't *gut* for the *boppli*."

He glanced over his shoulder and Susanna understood. A group of women had dressed Eve's body for burial two days earlier. Because Eve was so emaciated and had been dead several weeks now, there had been no viewing. But laying down the dirt to cover her grave was the last service Seth could perform for his wife on this earth. It was logical for him to assist in this final act.

"Of course." She took Miriam, careful not to awaken the baby. "We will see you over at the bishop's farm."

Seth nodded and turned to pick up a shovel. Susanna stood there a moment, surprised to see him brush at his eyes. As a rule, the Amish rarely showed overt emotions at a funeral. Rather, they accepted *Gott*'s will with faith and tolerance.

Without a word to the other men, Seth scraped the spade into the mound of dirt, scooped up some soil and tossed it into the gaping maw below. Again and again, each man took turns filling in the hole. The soil struck the coffin below with a hollow thud, the sound mirroring Susanna's heart.

Seth's brief show of emotion touched her heart like nothing else could. No doubt he had loved Eve very much and, once again,

Susanna wished her own husband had loved her even half as much.

Turning, she stepped over clumps of dried grass as she headed toward the waiting buggy, holding Miriam tightly in her arms, protecting her from the cold and damp. Through the rain-spattered windshield, she could see *Mammi* sitting inside, hunched tight as she wrapped herself in a warm quilt.

How sad that Thomas and Eve never realized their many blessings and overcame their addictions to live a happy life. Instead, they had made their spouses and families absolutely miserable with their actions. If only they had comprehended how much everyone wanted to love and cherish them. If only they had understood how much the Lord loved them, too. Maybe it would have given them the strength to overcome and make a difference for all of them.

Maybe not.

Although these thoughts filled Susanna with a melancholy she hadn't felt since her own husband's funeral, she realized she must not judge others. Not even Thomas. That was *Gott*'s burden and not hers. Instead, she must forgive and focus on her work.

Starting next week, she would open her noodle store with haste. The packages of pasta were already wrapped and ready to move over to the shop. If the summer months were productive enough, Susanna might be able to hire a part-time employee next fall to help with the work. In the meantime, she would fold little Miriam into her daily life and lose her regrets in hard labor.

Seth would learn to live with the disappointment of a lost marriage, just as Susanna had done. She must not make his troubles her own. Other than renting his building and looking after his child, Seth meant nothing to her. Susanna must not let her relationship with the man become more than what it was. An acquaintance. A member of her congregation. A landlord. Nothing more.

"Ach, that Susanna Glick is a right *gut* girl."

Seth tossed a shovelful of dirt onto his wife's coffin and looked up. Darrin Albrecht, the deacon of their congregation, stood leaning against the handle of his spade. Pushing back his black felt hat, the man jutted his chin at Susanna as she stepped gingerly over the other gravesites in the yard until she reached the rock path leading out of the cemetery. The other men all paused and stared after her, drops of rain dripping from the brims of their black felt hats. With some amusement, Seth wondered what Susanna would say if she could hear their conversation right now. He doubted she'd be pleased.

"*Ja*, and she's recently widowed herself," Mervin Schwartz, another elder of their church, spoke as he tossed a spade full of soil into the hole. "She has no *kinder* of her own, yet she seems mighty taken with your little Miriam. Susanna's a hard worker, too. And a *gut* cook and homemaker, from what I've heard. A kind, faithful woman. You should marry her, Seth. She'd make a fine wife and *mudder* to your *kinder*. She's the kind of woman who can make you forget your grief."

Seth gaped at the two men, thinking they had lost their minds. Here he was, literally burying his dead wife, and they had the audacity to suggest he marry someone else. To Seth, the notion was irreverent and unthinkable.

And very practical.

"I think right now, I'm going to finish laying my wife to rest and then return to the bishop's farm and enjoy a hearty lunch." Speaking firmly, Seth lowered his head as he scooped up another shovelful of dirt, trying to keep the anger out of his voice.

After all, wrath was not of the Lord. Seth knew these men meant well but his heart was fractured. How could he ever think about re-marrying now, when the wounds Eve had inflicted on him were still so raw and painful? He couldn't! Not ever again.

"I'm sorry, Seth. I didn't mean any harm," Mervin said.

The man clasped Seth's shoulder, his gaze filled with contrition.

"It's *allrecht*," Seth reassured him.

He understood the gravity of his own situation. With a child to raise and a farm to run, he needed to marry again as soon as possible. But what he needed and what his heart would allow were two different things. Besides, it would not be fair to marry a woman he didn't love. Not to her and not to him. He had tried that with Eve and look how it all turned out.

"*Ne*, it is not *allrecht*. I should be more sensitive. But you see, I went through something like this with my first wife, too. And I hate to see you so unhappy," Mervin said.

Seth gazed at the older man, stunned and hardly able to do more than blink. "You... you did?"

Mervin nodded as he tossed more earth onto the grave. "*Ja*, most folks don't remember anymore that I was married once before. Ellen was awfully pretty but she had a rebellious heart and I lost her to the world. She was shunned by our people for adultery, just like your Eve."

Wow! Seth had no idea. But he was relatively new to the area and hadn't yet heard this story.

The group of men kept up with their task but Seth knew they were listening to every word. They each took their turn at filling in the grave as Mervin told them more.

"Shortly after we wed, Ellen ran off with an *Englisch* man. She said she wanted to divorce me but she never did. You know our people don't hold with that kind of thing anyway. I had resigned myself to never being able to marry again as long as Ellen was alive. Then, I received word that she'd died with her *boppli* in childbirth and the *Englisch* man she'd taken up with was nowhere to be found. He'd abandoned her when she needed him the most. Of course, the *boppli* wasn't mine but I stepped in to see that he and Ellen received a proper burial. It nearly broke my heart but she was still my wife and I had to do right by her. I knew it was no less than what the Lord expected from me."

Feeling the burn of tears, Seth looked away. He didn't speak but focused on his labors instead. He couldn't believe that Mervin understood exactly what he was going through. The anger and pain he tried so hard to push aside. The tenets of his faith dictated that he must not be upset. That he must not be angry. It was *Gott*'s place to judge Eve, not his. He must accept the Lord's will. It was on the tip of his tongue to confess that he didn't believe Miriam was his child, either. But he bit the words back and held his silence. He could never hurt Miriam by revealing the truth. Maybe not now, but later on down the road she would hear about it. And he did not want her to feel any worse about her mother's passing than she needed to. Because they knew about Eve's adultery, some people in his *Gmay* may have figured it out but they would never speak it out loud unless he did first.

"But you married Hannah and raised a large *familye* with her," Caleb Burkholder, another older member of their congregation, pointed out.

Mervin nodded and showed a satisfied smile. "*Ja*, I did, indeed. Marrying my Hannah was the smartest decision I ever made. I met her shortly after Ellen died. I didn't think

I could ever love again but I was wrong. My Hannah has been a beauty and a blessing in my life, just as Sarah was to the prophet Abraham." He looked at Seth and his eyes crinkled with compassion. "Don't give up hope, Seth. Love will *komm* your way again. I know you are hurting right now but, if you have faith and hold firm to *Gott*'s will, I promise you will find happiness again one day when you least expect it to happen."

Seth snorted. He couldn't stop himself. The negativity just burst out of him.

"Not today," he said. "I appreciate your kind words but I am not going to marry Susanna Glick, or anyone. Not ever again. Now, if you will excuse me, I am cold, wet and tired, just like you. I am going back to the bishop's farm to see my *dochder* and enjoy a warm meal. Tomorrow is another day and I have got a farm to run. That's all I am going to think about for now."

Bringing the flat of his shovel down hard on top of the newly filled-in grave, he smacked it several times to tamp down the loose soil. Then, he shoved the blade into the dirt at the side of the headstone and turned and walked away in the drizzling rain.

He didn't look back at the men but he knew

they were standing there, watching him go. His heart felt numb and deadened with anguish. Yet, he knew these brethren were his friends. They had all come to his farm and harvested his potatoes, just as he would have done for them if the situation was reversed. They cared about him and wanted his success. But he couldn't offer them any hope that he would ever marry Susanna. She had obviously loved Thomas, her first husband. When she finally remarried, she deserved that kind of adoring relationship again. And he could never give it to her. Not now, not ever. Not after all that had happened with Eve. He would never trust another woman with his heart again. And that was that.

Chapter Five

As planned, Susanna pulled her horse and wagon to a halt out front of Seth's empty store the following week. It was early, the sun barely peeking over the Wet Mountains. Gray clouds filled the sky, promising a cold, drizzly day. But with her crop of potatoes gathered in, she didn't care. Now, it was time to focus on her noodle business.

Taking a deep, settling breath, Susanna glanced up and saw a vague light gleaming from one of the windows in the apartment overhead. Not surprising. Either Seth was inside tending to the baby's needs or out in the barn seeing to his morning chores. Most Amish got up around four o'clock each morning to feed their livestock and tend to other work before eating breakfast and sending their children off to school and their men out to the fields. It was a farmer's life. Susanna and *Mammi* were no exception, but they had no kids or menfolk of their own.

Looking over at her grandmother, Susanna could barely see the older woman among the boxes and bags crowding the front seat of the wagon. More boxes filled with packages of pasta, sacks of flour and heavy mixing equipment were in the back. Everything they needed to make and sell their handmade noodles.

A flutter of delight filled her stomach and she took a deep, cleansing breath. She had dreamed of this day all her life but never believed it would actually come to fruition. Now that she was truly opening her own store, she could hardly believe it was really happening. She had never felt more independent in her life and the sensation was giddy and exhilarating.

"Are you ready?" *Mammi* peeked around a box, her voice filled with cheerful exuberance. No doubt she was excited, too.

"*Ja*, I think so. We packed everything but the kitchen sink."

"*Ne*, I think that is in here somewhere, too," *Mammi* teased with a smile.

Chuckling, Susanna hopped out of the buggy and hurried around to assist her grandma. Her heart thudded with anticipation, gratitude and a bit of trepidation. After all, she had never done this before. She hated the thought of going to Bishop Yoder to ask for financial assistance. What if this didn't work out? What if no one came to the shop to buy her noodles?

No! She must not think that way. Running a business wouldn't be easy but she was not afraid of hard work. She was determined to make this a success. Her financial independence rested on it.

Reaching up, Susanna took hold of *Mammi*'s arm as the elderly woman stepped down carefully. With the cold weather, *Mammi*'s rheumatism was acting up. She moved stiffly, as if her back, legs and ankles didn't want to bend.

"Why don't you go on inside? I will unload everything and you can help me put it all away," Susanna suggested.

"Nonsense! I'm here to work," *Mammi* said. "And I have noticed, when I keep moving, it eases the aches in my body. So, don't you try to stop me from helping out. I will not be put on a shelf."

Susanna nodded, unwilling to argue with her grandmother's stern logic. Though she worried about *Mammi*, she also had great respect for her. And if *Mammi* said she wanted to work, then *Mammi* meant it.

A spatula dropped to the ground as *Mammi* grappled with a box of baking utensils she pulled from the wagon. A tower of cardboard wobbled precariously beside them. Using her shoulder and chest to block any other items from falling out, Susanna took the box from *Mammi* and waited as her grandmother stabilized the pile.

"Can you squeeze past me?" Susanna asked.

"Just barely." *Mammi* inched away from the wagon, then pressed her hands against a twenty-five-pound bag of flour to keep it from tipping forward.

With the stack steadied for the moment, Susanna laughed. "Goodness, this is quite a load. I don't think we could have gotten one more thing inside this wagon."

"That is for certain…"

"Here, Dorothy. That's too heavy for you. Let me take it."

Susanna jerked as strong hands reached past her to clasp the heavy bag of flour. Whirling around, she was startled to find Seth standing close beside her. As he hefted the bag onto his shoulder with ease, Susanna scurried out of his way. *Mammi* did likewise, smiling with appreciation.

"*Ach*, Seth! You startled me." Dorothy clasped her hands together in delight.

The man simply ducked his head and carried the flour sack into the building. Susanna followed, struggling with her own heavy tub of dishes, dishcloths and towels. She had barely made it through the front door when Seth appeared from the kitchen and tried to take the burden from her.

"Let me help," he said.

"*Ne*, I have it," she said, evading his grasp as she rushed into the back storeroom.

She didn't glance at him but, out of her peripheral vision, she caught his look of surprise. It didn't matter. She could not bring herself to accept his assistance. Her freedom was too important to her. Right now, her response was physical. Her body tensed and plunged forward of its own volition, a defensive instinct to do it herself.

Inside the pantry, she set the tub down with a light thud. Taking a deep breath, she tried to settle her nerves.

"Susanna?"

She whirled around and found him standing in the doorway, holding two boxes in his strong arms. For a scant moment, she could only stare at him, wishing he would go away.

"Where do you want these things?" he asked.

Mentally shaking herself, she hurried forward.

"Just set them there for now." She pointed at the wall where the boxes would be out of the way for the time being. "*Mammi* and I will sort everything out later as we put it all away."

He set the boxes on the floor, then raked his fingers through his long hair. He was in bad need of a haircut but she didn't offer to take care of it for him. Right now, she had other pressing matters on her mind.

"Looks like you brought everything," he said, a half smile curving his handsome mouth. "When are you planning to officially open the store for business?"

She stepped out into the kitchen, her gaze taking in the pristine cleanliness of the room. Her fingers almost itched to get started making a batch of dough right now. But first things first.

"Hopefully as soon as tomorrow. It depends on how quickly we can get the shelves stocked with our pasta. They're all packaged and ready to sell but I want the displays to look nice. I've got some signs to put up, too. But first, I'm sure you are eager to get to work. Where is Miriam?" she asked.

He tilted his face and looked up at the ceiling. "She's upstairs. I bathed her early this morning and took her out to the barn with me to milk the goats. She loved it. But I have not fed her, yet. I'm afraid she is rather hungry. She's had a bottle but nothing else to eat. Would you mind feeding her?"

Susanna dusted her hands before wiping them on the practical black apron tied around her waist. "*Ach*, of course. I will see to that right now. Boxes can wait when there is a hungry *boppli* needing food. You go on and head out to the barn. Don't worry. We will take *gut* care of her."

He gave one nod. "I know you will. While you feed the *boppli*, I will finish unloading your wagon, then take your horse around back and put him in the barn with my livestock until you are ready to go *heemet* later this evening."

She blinked, thinking this over. Why wouldn't he just go away?

"You don't need to unload my wagon. I can manage," she said.

He was already turning toward the front door. "It will not take but a few minutes and then it will be done. Besides, if I don't help you out, Dorothy will do it. And I would rather take the load on myself. She is rather frail and I don't want her injured."

So. He had noticed. How perceptive and considerate of him.

Watching him go, Susanna felt suspicious. He was right, of course. For all of her objections to being coddled, *Mammi* was older and feeble now. Susanna didn't want the woman to overdo it. But Seth's insight and concern were so new to her. Thomas had never offered his aid without an ulterior motive. He never went out of his way to help others, either. Not without asking something in return. He would act kind but always seemed to have a hidden agenda. Susanna just hoped Seth was not of the same ilk.

Heading toward the long hallway leading to the apartment above, she hurried up the stairs. Like the last time she was here, she found Miriam sitting in her playpen, her empty bottle lying beside her. She was quietly playing with a wooden horse. Most Amish men were good with their hands, making furniture and carving wood. Susanna had no doubt Seth had made the toy for his daughter.

At first sight of her, Miriam released that breathless gasp of hers and gave a cute little squeal of joy. She smiled wide and dropped the horse as she reached out her arms.

Susanna's heart turned a somersault. Picking up the girl, she couldn't help kissing her velvety-soft cheek as she carried the baby into the kitchen.

"*Hallo, Liebchen.* Are you hungry?" she asked as she went.

Miriam babbled enthusiastically as Susanna set her in her high chair and handed her a chunk of banana to chew on while she made some oatmeal and a fresh bottle. In the process, Susanna washed the pile of dishes in the sink and wiped down the counters and table. While the baby ate, she quickly scooped grimy clothes into a black garbage bag to launder later on, then she swept and mopped the floors and scrubbed the toilet and bathroom sink. The chores took only a matter of minutes but made all the difference in tidying the apartment.

As she worked, Susanna thought about all the tasks awaiting her downstairs and a sense of urgency built within her chest. But she could never begrudge Miriam or her *vadder.* The baby was without her mom and needed someone to look after her. And since the child needed time to eat, it took little effort to keep working in the meantime. Because of her agreement with Seth, Susanna was now able to set up her store and hopefully branch out to sell her pasta in other towns. She just needed time and patience. And along the way, she would tend this baby like she was her own. Miriam deserved nothing less.

Forty minutes later, Susanna carried the child downstairs and was both pleased and surprised to find all her boxes and equipment waiting for her in the outer store and kitchen areas. A glance out the front window told her Seth had done as promised and taken her horse and wagon to the barn. And because he had completed these things for her, she was right on schedule even with cleaning his apartment.

Mammi was methodically emptying a box as she filled the shelves with beautifully packaged pastas. Each bag looked delicious, quaint and professionally done.

"*Ach*, you have gotten a lot finished while I've been upstairs." Susanna laughed, once again grateful to Seth for his help.

Mammi shrugged, her eyes sparkling as a satisfied smile curved her lips. "*Ja*, I figure we should have our shelves stocked and be able to open the store by tomorrow morning. Thanks to Seth. While you were tending the *boppli*, he unloaded our entire wagon. He is such a nice young man. I really like him, Susanna."

Yes, but maybe he was too nice. Thomas

had acted the same way…at first. After their wedding, she had learned it was all a facade.

Susanna just smiled, saying nothing. *Mammi* always said that proof was in the pudding. If Seth was anything like Thomas, his true self would eventually show and she would see it soon enough.

She brought the playpen downstairs and set it on the floor, then placed the baby inside with some toys to occupy her. If only they didn't have to see or deal with Seth, things would be almost perfect. But it could not be helped. She didn't resent the man. Not when he had been so generous to her. But she felt mighty uncomfortable with his presence. It seemed they were stuck with each other. For now, she would offer a prayer of thanks and focus on her work. Part of her chores were looking after *Mammi* and Miriam. She could accept that. But that did not mean she had to be any more deferential toward Seth.

By late afternoon, Seth was ravenous. Knowing Miriam was being taken care of, he had accomplished a lot more than usual and worked right through lunch, clearing out his vegetable garden and picking the last of his tomatoes and apples from his two trees. The growing season was extra short here in Colorado. Now, he had two bushels of tomatoes, nine bushels of golden delicious apples and no idea how to bottle them.

If he had time, he was going to build a large greenhouse for next year. But honestly, he didn't know why he bothered. Eve had never been interested in growing things, an oddity for an Amish woman. But Seth loved fresh fruits and vegetables. It was the food he had been raised on as a boy. He just wasn't prepared to bottle what he grew. In the past, Eve had preserved a few cases by enlisting friends from their congregation to help with the chore. He had no idea what the bottling process entailed.

He had seen his mom and other women preserving peaches, pears, string beans, corn and anything else they could get their hands on every fall as they harvested what they raised. Short of husking the corn and shelling pinto beans, most menfolk didn't participate in the kitchen work. He could not imagine hiring one of the Amish women in his congregation to bottle for him. But what choice did he have? He needed a food supply to live. Maybe he could ask Susanna and Dorothy if they would be willing to do the chore in exchange for payment.

Stepping inside his shed, he hung his shovel,

hoe and rake on the wall, then took inventory of his seeds for next year's garden. He was low on carrots, beets and peas. He had plenty of potatoes in his food supply but thought he should buy cases of canned vegetables and fruit from the general store. He had grown and used a lot of produce this past summer but had not bottled a thing. Usually a vegetable garden was tended by the woman of the house. Because Eve didn't do the chore consistently, he'd resorted to caring for it himself, but it added to his workload. He was on his own. He would have to figure it out. One day at a time.

As he secured the door and headed toward the store, he paused at the water hydrant in his backyard. Tugging on the spigot, he rinsed off the mud beneath the gush of water. Shaking off his hands to dry them, he headed toward the back door.

Looking up, he paused, surprised to see various miniature baby dresses, black tights, blankets and sheets hanging on the clothesline. Even a pair of his broadfall pants, undergarments and several shirts waved in the chilly breeze. Susanna and her grandma must have washed his laundry. He had not expected this and a feeling of embarrassment flooded him.

Slipping inside, he entered the kitchen.

With her back toward him, Dorothy stood at the sink, washing dishes. The yummy smell of something good baking in the oven filled the air and his stomach rumbled. He hadn't thought the women would prepare their meals here but it was not his business. The bottom part of the building had been let out to Susanna, including the kitchen. No doubt, the two women were so busy setting up their store that they had decided to take their meals here. It definitely was more convenient than driving back and forth to their farmhouse to eat.

Glancing to the side, Dorothy smiled wide. "*Hallo*, Seth. I didn't see you there. Are you finished with your garden work?"

He nodded, knowing she had a perfect view of his backyard from the window over the kitchen sink. No doubt she had watched him clearing the field of dead plants before he spread a layer of compost to set throughout the long winter months.

"*Ja*, I got it all cleaned out and picked my apples, too."

"*Gut!* Susanna did our garden last week but we don't have any apple trees. Are you finished with your chores for the day?"

"*Ne*, I've still got the milking and feeding

my livestock to do. Then, I thought I would spend a little time with Miriam."

Dorothy rinsed and dried a large, clean bowl before setting it aside on the gleaming stainless steel counter. She jutted her chin toward the stairs leading to his apartment above. "Susanna took the *boppli* upstairs about twenty minutes ago. Miriam has had a busy day, too. She was pretty worn out and needed a bottle and a nap."

He nodded and stepped into the hallway. From his vantage point, he could see into the store area and was drawn there against his will. At first sight, he could hardly believe the transformation. The boxes he had unloaded earlier that morning were gone. All the shelves were now filled with the prettiest packages of handmade noodles, spaghetti and other pastas he had ever seen. One shelf showed a variety of jarred pasta sauces…red, white, green, spicy and mild. A charming display near the front door showed a weekly special on spaghetti… Buy three packages and get a jar of sauce for free.

He reached down and lifted one package of noodles off a shelf. It was labeled with a stocking number, price and ingredients. Very professional and well done. Obviously, Susanna and her grandmother had done a lot of prep work before they arrived at the store early that morning. He'd been skeptical that they would be ready to open tomorrow for business, but even the Open/Closed sign in the front window showed that he was wrong.

As he looked around the room and saw that everything was in its place, he felt more than impressed. Susanna and her grandmother had done all of this, in addition to caring for his baby and washing his laundry. Susanna didn't mess around, that was for sure. When she said she was going to do something, she did it. Fast. And he could not help wishing Eve had acquired even a fraction of Susanna's initiative.

Shaking his head, he returned to the hallway and took hold of the handrail. He walked upstairs quietly, so he would not awaken Miriam if she was asleep.

As he stepped into the main living area of his home, he froze. Like the store below, everything was tidy and in its place. Gone were the piles of dirty dishes and clothes he had left for later. The broken leather halter he'd been mending the night before lay on the floor beside the door…a silent indication that it belonged out in the barn, not in his living room. The scent of pine cleaner made his nose twitch and he was certain the floors had been mopped. The coffee table and gas-powered lamps gleamed. It appeared that Susanna had cleaned his home, too.

A faint sound caught his ear and he turned toward the hallway. Someone was humming a sweet lullaby.

Stepping over to his daughter's bedroom, he peeked around the corner. With her back to him, Susanna sat in the rocking chair he had made for Eve as a gift when Miriam was first born. He had hoped that having a baby might keep his wife home for good, but it had not influenced Eve one single bit. Now, Susanna was cuddling his little daughter close in her arms as she rocked back and forth, singing quietly to the girl. Silently, he shifted his angle so he could see his daughter better. Miriam's eyes were closed, her little rosebud lips making a gentle sucking motion. The baby looked perfectly healthy and content.

An overwhelming emotion filled Seth as he stared at this stranger snuggling his daughter. For three years, he had tried to have this kind of life with Eve, but she had refused. In the beginning, he had loved Eve and still could not understand why she'd pushed him and Miriam away. Why she would not do the hard work to overcome her addictions and save their marriage…and save her own life, too. If not for him, at least she owed it to her daughter. But it seemed Eve would not make an effort. Not even when he'd tried to get her some help from a professional doctor at the hospital. She had flatly refused to go. And recounting this in his mind just renewed the pain and regrets that haunted his heart.

Susanna leaned her head down and kissed the baby's forehead. As she slowly rose from the rocking chair and laid Miriam gently in her crib, Seth pulled back before she saw him spying on her. As he hurried to the kitchen, his stomach growled hungrily. He opened the gas-powered refrigerator, wondering what he could make for his supper. He was kneeling down in front of the crisper, searching for a potato, when Susanna joined him.

"*Ach*, Seth! I didn't know you were here," she said.

He stood and closed the fridge, resigned to opening a can of store-bought beef stew. It wasn't homemade, but it was filling.

Facing her, he showed a half-smile. She stepped back, as if she was trying to keep her distance from him.

"*Ja*, I thought I would make something to eat," he said, feeling foolish and inept.

The few times Eve had cooked for him, she'd prepared the tastiest meals. But Seth had never been much good at the chore. He could make basics to keep himself going but greatly missed the home-cooked meals his mom had prepared in his youth.

Susanna lifted a hand toward the hallway. "I just fed and put Miriam down for a nap. You won't want to let her sleep more than an hour, though. Otherwise, she will keep you up late tonight."

He chuckled. "*Ja*, I have learned that lesson the hard way. Most of the time, Miriam is happy and sweet. But in the middle of the night, she has got a fierce temper and a strong pair of lungs."

Susanna laughed, too, the sound high, sweet and almost alien to him. He couldn't remember the last time he'd heard Eve laugh.

"I can just imagine that," she said.

Every coherent thought fled his mind and all he could do was stare at Susanna. She blinked, as if remembering her chores downstairs, then inched toward the door, seeming eager to escape.

"*Ach*, I had better get back to the kitchen. We are winding down our workday and need to head home so we can care for our own farm. Do you need me to look after Miriam anymore tonight?"

"I… I don't think so. I can take it from here," he said.

"Susanna! Seth! Supper is ready. *Komm* and eat while it's hot," Dorothy called from below.

Seth blinked. He had not expected an invitation to eat.

Giving a nervous laugh, Susanna hurried toward the exit. "*Ach*, I guess *Mammi* has got everything ready for us. You better *komm* now."

And just like that, she was gone. He could hear her light footsteps as she hurried down the stairs, then her and Dorothy's low voices filtering from below. He was tempted to remain right where he was and figure something out for his own meal. But honestly, the tantalizing aroma of Dorothy's cooking had wafted up to his apartment and he was ravenous enough that he could not bring himself to refuse such a wonderful offer.

Leaving the apartment door wide open so he could hear Miriam if she awoke, he joined Dorothy and Susanna for their evening meal.

When she saw him standing in the doorway, Dorothy pulled a chair back from the wide counter. "Sit here, Seth."

He stepped over to take his place, noticing she had laid out three plates and utensils. But there were no more seats.

"*Ne*, you sit. I will bring two more chairs down from my apartment," he said, disappearing before the women could argue the point.

He returned moments later, just as Susanna was pulling what looked to be a chicken and rice casserole out of the oven. With a quick twist of her wrist, she turned off the appliance. After setting the steaming pan on a hot pad she'd placed on the counter, she reached for a basket of fresh rolls. Dorothy placed a bowl of corn beside a dish of butter and one of raspberry jam. The food smelled lovely.

"Wow! This looks delicious. *Danke* for inviting me," Seth said.

Dorothy jerked a thumb toward Susanna. "Don't thank me. Susanna made our supper tonight."

He glanced at Susanna, whose cheeks suddenly flushed a pretty shade of pink. She took her seat, then ducked her head and folded her hands, anticipating prayer. Dorothy did likewise. When they finished, Seth waited patiently for Susanna to dish up a plate of food for each of them. His stomach rumbled impatiently and he pressed a hand over his abdomen.

"It sounds like you are hungry. Dig in. Hard work builds up a hearty appetite," Dorothy said as she passed him the bowl of corn.

He gave a nervous laugh as he reached for three rolls. "It sure does. I forgot to eat lunch today, so this meal is a blessing."

"*Ach*, you had no lunch?" Dorothy made a tsking sound and shook her head. "That settles it. You will take your lunch and supper with us from now on."

"Oh, *ne*! I can't impose on you like that," Seth said, thinking it was asking too much of them.

Dorothy scowled. "Why not? We are all busy and we all have to eat. I can't do a lot of the heavy lifting but I can sure cook. You will eat here with us and that is the end of it."

Seth stared at the two women, noticing Susanna was overly quiet. And suddenly, he wondered if this arrangement was a huge mistake. He could not put his finger on why, but Susanna didn't seem to like him. She obviously was not comfortable around him. And yet, he couldn't help admiring her work ethic and skills.

Dorothy gave a knowing nod and glanced

at Susanna. "Seth got his vegetable garden cleared and picked his apples today."

Susanna did not even look up as she took a bite of food. "That's *gut*."

"I told him we got our garden cleaned up last week but we have no apples," Dorothy continued, obviously trying hard to make conversation.

"I have two bushels of overly ripe tomatoes," he said.

Dorothy lifted one eyebrow. "*Ach*, is that right?"

"*Ja*, I… I was wondering if… Would it be too much of an imposition if I paid you extra to bottle them when you do your own? Most of my apples will keep but not the tomatoes," Seth said.

There. That was good. No handouts. He had offered to pay them for their work.

Susanna hesitated, holding her fork aloft as she gazed at him. She opened her mouth to speak but no sound issued forth. Perhaps it was the way her forehead crinkled in a frown, but he sensed she was about to refuse. He could see something in her eyes…a mixture of suspicion and doubt.

"Of course, we would love to do it," Dorothy said. "And no need to pay us for the task.

We have already bottled our produce but it wouldn't be difficult to do yours as well. I can bottle the tomatoes tomorrow, right here in this kitchen, while Susanna minds the front of the store. Let me bottle some of your apples, too. They will keep longer than the tomatoes and I can bottle them over the next few weeks as I find the time. You can keep some for eating and I will turn several bushels into applesauce for the *boppli* and some sliced apples for pies, too."

Susanna's eyes widened as she looked at her grandmother. But she didn't say a word. Just ducked her head and took another forkful of tasty rice into her mouth.

"Are you sure you would not mind doing all of that?" Seth asked, feeling skeptical as he looked back and forth between the two women.

"Not at all. I enjoy bottling. It gives me a sense of comfort knowing our shelves are stocked with food for the winter. It will be fine, won't it, Susanna?" Dorothy said, her voice filled with pleasant insistence.

"*Ja*, just fine," Susanna said, not meeting his eyes.

Seth bit into a warm, buttered roll. It tasted so good, he almost groaned with pleasure.

"I… I am happy to see you got your store set up. Are you opening for business tomorrow, then?" he asked.

A light of satisfaction flickered in Susanna's eyes and she smiled so bright that he had to blink.

"*Ja*, I think we are ready. I am going to make some handouts to post around town to help us advertise. Hopefully, we will get some customers coming in before too long," she said.

As she looked at him, her smile faded and she returned her attention to her plate. And once again, he got the impression she felt uncomfortable around him. He wasn't sure why. He had never been rude to her. Never raised a hand or acted anything but polite when she was near. Maybe she was disgusted by him because of all the gossip surrounding him and Eve. Maybe she even blamed him for Eve's death. He honestly did not know.

They didn't speak much after that and he ate in silence. The meal was delicious and he accepted a huge wedge of apple pie for dessert. He was not surprised when Dorothy informed him that Susanna made the pie, too…from apples they'd bottled last season. It seemed she was good at everything she did.

The moment Susanna finished her meal,

she hopped up and began washing dishes. She was probably eager to get home to the chores awaiting her there. It was getting late and he must not detain them any longer.

The women soon made their departure and he went to check on Miriam. Another hour of chores and he could lie down and rest for the night. Then, they would all repeat their day tomorrow. One thing was certain. This life was filled with lots of hard work.

As he picked up Miriam and kissed her soft cheek, he noticed she smelled nice. He was surprised to discover that he looked forward to seeing Dorothy and Susanna again. Susanna was a bit offish with him, yet he still liked her a lot. He told himself it was just because he had been alone for so many years. For the most part, he really had no one he could talk to. In spite of being a married man, Eve had been gone a long time and he had been on his own with just Miriam to keep him company. But a feeling deep inside told him it was something more. He liked Susanna, which was very odd. Because she obviously did not return the sentiment. She clearly thought of their arrangement as nothing more than a business agreement. He doubted they would ever be more than distant friends.

Chapter Six

The bell over the shop door tinkled gaily, heralding the arrival of another customer. Susanna looked up and smiled as two *Englisch* women stepped inside the store. She had barely opened an hour earlier and had already sold enough merchandise to pay her grocery bill for the month. For a solid week now, business in the shop had been steady. The bright winter day was unseasonably warm but made it easy for people to visit her grand opening and she hoped her business became a raging success as the holiday months progressed.

"I will be right with you," she called in a pleasant voice, speaking in perfect English for the benefit of the shopper.

Gathering her composure, she pasted a smile on her face. After all, she was not used to so many *Englischers* at once and felt a bit shy doing business with them.

Holding Miriam against her hip with one arm, she stood in front of the old-fashioned cash register. *Mammi* had gone into town or Susanna would have let her tend the child. She had been worried about needing to help her customers with a baby in her arms but the *Englisch* people seemed to like it. Susanna suspected, because both she and Miriam were dressed in plain Amish clothes, the *Englischers* found them rather unique, quaint and charming. And if that was a helpful draw to bring people into her shop, Susanna didn't mind one bit.

Reaching for a decorative paper sack with her free hand, she rang up six bags of noodles and three jars of pasta sauce, placed them inside the sack, then accepted payment.

"Thank you. I hope you will come again soon." She smiled and spoke sweetly as the woman handed her sack of purchases to her husband, then nodded and left the store.

Closing the cash register drawer, Susanna immediately carried Miriam with her to wait on the new arrivals. It was a Saturday and the week had been hectic. For all of them.

While Susanna had looked after Miriam

and worked in the store, *Mammi* had bottled Seth's tomatoes, apples and applesauce in the kitchen. In return, Seth had spread manure in all the fields at Susanna's farm and repaired her combine machine for next season's planting. She had no idea what was wrong with the silly thing, but Seth seemed to understand perfectly. If not for him, she would have had to pay someone in town to fix it for her.

Seth had not told her he was going to do the chores. He had just done them. She'd discovered the freshly turned soil in her fields on Tuesday evening when she had gone home to feed her livestock. He'd done other things for her, too. Her husband had let their farm fall into disrepair. Susanna had been pleasantly surprised to discover Seth had mended her fence, corrals and shed, too. He had even overhauled her chicken coop so the hens couldn't get out at night and a fox couldn't get in. This kind of teamwork had not escaped her notice and she was impressed by Seth's consideration and diligence. In fact, she owed him a great debt of gratitude but did not want to thank him. He might get the wrong idea and think she was interested in him. And she wasn't. Not in a million years. Even if everyone in their congregation thought they would make a good match.

Now, Miriam clung to her arm, observing the goings-on inside the store with sober intensity. The baby was as quiet and good-natured as could be and the morning had flown by, with numerous shoppers frequenting the store.

"Ah, your baby is such a little cutie," one *Englisch* woman cooed at the child.

Susanna did not correct the lady's error. Miriam wasn't her baby but Susanna wished she was. Instead, she just pasted a smile on her face. "Good morning. What can I help you with today?"

The woman turned toward the shelves of various kinds of noodles and pastas before picking up a package of fettuccine. "How odd. Why are these noodles green? What's in them?"

"They're made with spinach, ma'am," Susanna replied in a respectful tone. "It does not have a heavy taste of spinach but the pasta is firm enough to stand up to a nice, robust sauce."

"Oh! I like that. And these? What are they made of?" The lady picked up a package of reddish-orange linguine.

"That is made with dried roasted tomatoes. The tomatoes really enhance the flavor of the pasta. It is quite delicious with a hearty red sauce."

The woman immediately placed the packages in the shopping basket hanging from her left arm. "And this one?"

"That's just a regular egg noodle. It goes beautifully in chicken soup or with this clam sauce."

Holding Miriam tight, Susanna bent at the waist and picked up a jar of creamy, white sauce she had ordered from a wholesale supplier several weeks earlier.

The woman barely glanced at the sauce but placed it in her basket before snatching up a second bottle. "Yes, I want that. My husband will love it for dinner tonight. And do you have any noodles made without whole eggs?"

"Yes, right here. This is made without yolks." Susanna stepped over to another shelf and picked up some pasta before pointing at the label. "All of the ingredients are displayed right here on the front of each package. I don't use preservatives."

The woman peered at the neatly typed words. Weeks earlier, Susanna had ordered her labels premade from a shop here in town. When she was ready, she just pulled the back off and stuck the label onto the front of the clear plastic packages of pasta. It made things quite simple for her and *Mammi*.

"Oh! How unique. No preservatives?" the woman asked with awe.

"*Ne*, ma'am. Most of my pasta is made with just egg, flour, water and a pinch of salt. Not too much, though. Too much salt isn't *gut* for us, either," Susanna said, smiling pleasantly.

"Well, I like that," the woman said, snatching up several more packages.

"Let me know if you need anything else." Susanna stepped away to give the woman room to shop.

Susanna was surprised at how easy it was to upsell her customers. She simply told them the truth about her pastas and which sauces might taste good with them, and the people snapped them up. At this rate, she would need to replenish her shelves more often than she first thought. Maybe she and *Mammi* would have to make dough three days per week instead of two.

As she stepped away, she glanced around the store to ensure her other two customers were finding what they needed. When she glanced toward the cash register, she froze.

Seth stood in the doorway leading to the kitchen. Holding his battered felt hat in front of him, he hung back, as if he didn't want to intrude. In a glance, she took in his plain, work-stained clothes, scuffed boots and black suspenders. He wore a hesitant, endearing expression. As if he was not quite sure what to do here. He showed a slight smile and shifted his feet nervously, as though he did not want to be seen. A jagged thatch of hair covered his high forehead and fell into his eyes. He pushed it back rather impatiently but it quickly returned.

Susanna walked over to him and Miriam immediately reached for her daddy.

"Da!" the baby cried with delight.

They both smiled as he pulled his daughter into his arms and held her close for several moments.

"She definitely knows your name," Susanna said, speaking in *Deitsch*.

"She sure does," he said, his voice filled with happy pride. Then, he nodded at the room. "It looks like you are busy again today."

Susanna turned to face the store, just in case one of her buyers needed her attention. "*Ja*, it has been a steady stream of customers all day. It rarely lets up. I am looking forward to a break tomorrow for the Sabbath."

So she and *Mammi* had time to take inventory and make more noodles, she had decided to close the store on Mondays. And of course, they shut their doors on Sundays, too. Nothing took precedence over attending church and worshipping *Gott*.

Her heart pounded with excitement. If only business could stay like this, she would soon be able to hire some part-time help.

"*Gut!* I'm happy for you, Susanna," he said.

She jerked her head up and looked at him. The way he said her name caused her heart to skip a beat. There was such approval and friendship in his tone that she felt suspicious of him. Was he as wonderful as he seemed? Or was he hiding a dark side? It didn't really matter because they were not married. She had finally gotten her independence and was not about to relinquish it to any man.

She stepped back and looked away. She was standing a bit too close to him. For a few minutes, she had forgotten herself and let down her guard.

He smelled of horses and peppermint and she thought perhaps he'd just eaten a piece of candy. Thomas had always smelled of tobacco and alcohol and she could not help comparing the two men. Her husband had seemed so angry and moody all the time. In contrast, Seth seemed filled with light, hard work and positive energy.

"Did you need something? Or were you just paying a visit to the *boppli*?" she asked.

"I was actually looking for Dorothy. Is she here, by chance?" He scanned the room for some sight of the elderly woman.

"*Ne*, she had to run a quick errand to the post office for me. I had several mail orders of pasta that needed to be sent out before they close. She will be back soon, though. Can I give her a message for you?"

He nodded and lifted a hand to rake his fingers through his overly long hair. "*Ja*, I was hoping she might give me a haircut later this afternoon. I can't stand this long hair a minute longer."

Susanna laughed. "I am sure she would cut it for you, but you would be sorry afterward."

He tilted his head, his eyes crinkled in a questioning look. Miriam was tugging on one of his suspenders and babbling in her cute little voice.

"*Mammi* is awfully shaky these days. I am afraid she's got palsy," Susanna explained. "She would do her best to give you a nice, even haircut but you might end up with a snipped car or two in the process. You had better let me cut it for you instead."

Oh, dear. The moment she made the offer,

she regretted it. She would need to bend close to him to snip the ends with her scissors and also run her fingers through his hair as she combed it. Such a chore seemed much too intimate and domestic for a woman who was purposefully avoiding men.

He chuckled, his hazel eyes sparkling with humor. "*Ach*, we can't have any snipped ears now, can we? Would you have time to cut it for me today? I am getting desperate enough that I have considered paying a visit to the barber in town. And I really don't want to do that, if I can help it."

She understood his reticence. Without a wife, mother or sister to cut his hair, it had gotten way too long. But he did not want to go to the *Englisch* barber, either. He was a nice enough man but might not understand their Amish ways. It would not do for Seth to show up at church on Sunday with a fancy haircut like most *Englisch* men wore.

Susanna nodded, noticing one of the shoppers was peering over a shelf to catch her eye. Reaching to take Miriam from him, Susanna briefly glanced at Seth as she spoke over her shoulder. "Of course, I will cut it for you. *Komm* into the store at closing time and I will take care of it right before we eat supper."

Without another word, she hurried over to help the customer. Immediately missing her daddy, Miriam fussed briefly but soon settled down as she was distracted by what was going on in the store. When Susanna looked up again, Seth was gone and she breathed a sigh of relief. Cutting his hair seemed like a rather personal task she did not want to do for him, but it couldn't be helped. With her shaky hands, *Mammi* would undoubtedly do a hack job on him. Susanna was determined not to overthink this. She would trim his hair as quickly as possible. It was a simple haircut, after all. Nothing more.

By early evening, Seth was ready to whack off his own hair. He had worked hard and felt filthy as he dusted his pants and shirt with his hands. After turning his two Percheron draft horses out into the corral, he headed toward his home. Bright lights gleamed from the kitchen downstairs and he had no doubt Dorothy and Susanna were inside preparing their evening meal. Somehow, knowing the two women were there with his little daughter brought him a sense of relief and comfort. For the first time in years, he wasn't all alone. When he let his guard down, he almost

felt like they were *familye*. But they weren't
and he had to remind himself constantly of
that fact.

The long hair falling over the back of his
shirt was damp with sweat. He hated the
thought of Susanna combing and cutting his
grimy hair. Maybe he could wash it before
suppertime.

Stepping inside, he could hear the two
women talking together in the kitchen. As
usual, the tantalizing aromas of cooking meat
and bread wafted through the air. Without a
word, he sidled down the hallway, then scurried up the stairs to his apartment above.
When he returned fifteen minutes later, he
was clean and ravenous for whatever the two
women had prepared for their evening meal.

"Guder owed," he called as he stepped into
the kitchen.

Susanna turned from the oven and nodded
as she lifted a large cast-iron skillet to the
stovetop. Though she was across the room, he
could see the gleam of golden-orange carrots,
peeled potatoes and a beautiful beef roast inside the pan. His stomach rumbled hungrily.

"Good evening," Dorothy called from
where she was setting plates and utensils on
the table.

"I am sorry I'm a bit late tonight," he said.

"It is no problem. We're running late, too. I think the meat and potatoes need a few more minutes before they are done." Susanna spooned drippings over the roast before sliding the pan back into the oven and closing the door.

"Supper looks *gut*." He stepped over to his daughter and pulled the baby free of her high chair.

Miriam reached up and smiled wide as she patted his cheek with one chubby little hand.

"Hi, darlin'. Did you have a *gut* day today?" he asked as he kissed her forehead.

A feeling of gratitude swept over him. How blessed he was to have this sweet little girl to greet him. She was a reminder of what he was working so hard for and that life was not all labor and drudgery. She was a token of something wonderful and fine in his world. A reason to get up every morning and fight on.

Removing the oven mitts from her hands, Susanna picked up a comb, a pair of scissors and a towel before gesturing to the outer door. "Let's cut your hair outside. I don't want to have to sweep up a mess inside tonight. Plus, I doubt the health inspector would like it either."

That's right. Seth had forgotten that this

kitchen was subject to occasional inspections by the health department. After all, Susanna was making and selling pasta to the public.

He nodded and handed Miriam over to Dorothy, who reached to take the baby from him.

"Danke," he said.

Dorothy just smiled, carrying the baby as she stepped over to the stove to stir a pan of what looked like smooth, brown gravy. Seth's mouth watered for the delicious food but his appetite would have to wait. He followed Susanna outside.

"Sit right here," Susanna said.

She pointed at a battered wooden chair resting beneath a tall elm tree devoid of leaves. A frosty breeze swept past and he shivered. Maybe he should have worn his jacket.

He sat and waited as she stood behind him. As she draped the towel around his shoulders and clipped it together at his throat with a clothespin, he did not move a muscle. It took all of his willpower not to look around at her as he felt her comb through his clean, damp hair. The snipping sounds of the scissors told him she had started cutting.

"I mended your galvanized watering trough today," he said, trying to make intelligent conversation.

"The one in my cow pasture?" she asked, leaning near as she trimmed the hair around his right ear. He felt her warm breath tickle against his cheek.

"*Ja*, the water level was down too low so I knew it must have sprung a leak. I had to empty all the water out, first. I used a nontoxic epoxy from the hardware store, so it should not hurt your livestock, but emptying the tank created a big mud puddle in your pasture. It should dry out by tomorrow afternoon. I heard in town that the weatherman is forecasting snow by the first of next week. I am hoping we get enough moisture for next summer's crops."

He was talking a lot and realized he was rather nervous with her standing so close to him.

"*Ja*, water is always a concern for us farmers," she said. "*Danke* for fixing the stock tank. In fact, I… I want to thank you for all you've done on my farm. You have looked after everything and been very kind."

Her words sounded rather timid and hesitant…as if it was difficult for her to say these things.

"You are *willkomm*. It's the least I can do after all you have done to help Miriam and me," he said.

She had moved around to face him, combing and clipping the bangs hanging into his eyes. He blinked as strands of his hair fluttered to the ground. The fabric of her skirt brushed against his knees. Bending at the waist, she looked so engrossed in her task, pressing the tip of her tongue against her upper lip…an endearing gesture that told him she was concentrating hard.

"It… It was our agreement. Tending Miriam is the rent I pay to use your building for my noodle shop," she said.

He snorted. "You have done a lot more than just look after Miriam for me."

She went very still, the scissors held in midair as she met his gaze. "Like what?"

It took him a moment to respond. For several profound moments, he felt engrossed by the dark, outer ring and golden irises of her amber-colored eyes.

"Um, like washing our laundry and cleaning our apartment. And Dorothy bottled all those tomatoes and apples for me, too. I've even been taking my meals with you. That is a big burden off my shoulders. I'm grateful to you for all of it," he said.

She waved her hand with the comb. "*Ach*, that's nothing. You have provided the meat and some vegetables. And besides, the *boppli* needed clean clothes and, since we were doing our own laundry anyway, it was no extra work to toss your things in as well. And we all have to eat. It is just logical for you to take your meals with us."

"Well, *danke* just the same. It has made a huge difference in my workload," he said. "Miriam and I are eating better, too. I'm sure it is not easy on you, taking care of your farm with your husband gone."

She went very still again. Then, she looked away, resuming her task. Maybe he should not have mentioned Thomas. She undoubtedly missed the man. And for a moment, Seth realized he missed Eve, too. Or at least, he missed the few good times they had shared. He mourned what they could have been together. He missed the dream of what they might have shared and what they might have meant to one another. But what he did not miss was the constant drama Eve had created in his life. The legal and financial difficulties she had caused had become almost unbearable. Now, his heart was filled with nothing but guilt and regrets.

As Susanna continued cutting his hair, he caught her subtle fragrance. A fresh, clean mixture of soap and baking that he quite liked. And in that moment, he realized Eve usually smelled like a medicine cabinet. He suspected the drugs and alcohol she consumed were coming out through her skin. She'd become so dependent upon the drugs that she had stopped eating or bathing regularly, too.

"I hope I didn't overstep by changing your shed and the barn when I mended the holes in the walls. I thought my configuration would work more efficiently," he said.

She paused a moment, then her quiet, thoughtful voice wafted over the rustling breeze blowing in from the north. "*Ne*, everything you have done has been perfect. It's just what we needed. Thomas never seemed to find time to mend the fences…or the hole in the wall. He was always too busy doing… other things."

Like what? Seth wondered. What could be more important than looking after your farm? A draft could make the livestock ill, especially during the cold season. An Amish family's livelihood was dependent upon the well-being of their animals and crops. If there was a huge hole in the barn wall, you fixed it. If the watering trough had a leak, you repaired it. Quick! Animals had to drink every day. Ignoring such problems led to dead stock, loss of money and no food for the winter. That was not the Amish way.

"How did that gaping hole get there, anyway? It looked like someone drove a piece of machinery through the barn wall," he said.

Susanna sighed, as if she didn't want to answer. "Thomas, he, um, was inebriated one night and accidentally drove the tractor through the wall."

What? Accidentally? How did a man unintentionally drive a tractor through his barn wall?

Seth had never heard about this before. Nor had he known that Thomas drank alcohol enough to become intoxicated.

He blinked, thinking maybe he had not known Thomas at all. Since the Amish in Colorado were less stringent than some districts in the east, a couple of them used tractors that had been adapted for off-road use only. The vehicles provided extra power for certain farm chores. They had steel tires that functioned well in a field but could not be driven on the roads for traveling. So, once Thomas had created the hole in the barn, why hadn't he repaired the wall?

"I hope no one was injured in the accident," he said.

"Um, *ne*, he was fine. I was inside the house when it happened. He was just a bit angry at the time."

Angry? That was not something the Amish people condoned either. Losing your temper enough to drive a tractor through a wall sounded pretty serious to Seth, but he didn't say so. It was not for him to judge. After all, Thomas was dead, so there was no need to report the incident to the bishop.

Susanna looked away but not before Seth caught an edge of disgust in her voice. From the bright color of her cheeks, she was embarrassed to speak about it, too. But surely that couldn't be. She had loved Thomas. Hadn't she? But maybe things were not always as they appeared.

"*Ach*, I am finished." She whipped the towel off his shoulders and gave it several hard shakes to disperse the hair. Then, she stepped back and gazed at him with a critical expression. "It looks nice and even. While I help *Mammi* put supper on the table, why don't you take a look in the mirror? If there is more you would like taken off, or if I cut something unevenly, I can quickly fix it for you. Then, we can eat."

He nodded. *"Allrecht. Danke."*

She turned and went inside. He followed, going into the bathroom to stare at himself in the tiny mirror he kept there. The Amish didn't condone primping or gazing at oneself in mirrors for long periods of time. They believed it led to too much *Hochmut*, the pride of the world. But from what Seth could tell, Susanna had done a fine job. As he ran his fingers through his shortened hair, it felt good to have the scratchy stuff off the back of his neck and out of his eyes.

He joined the women in the kitchen for their evening meal, still thinking about what Susanna had said. Thomas had neglected his farm. Seth had seen that for himself. From afar, everything looked fine. But once he started digging into the plowing, planting and repairs, Seth realized things had been ignored. The disrepair had not occurred just since Thomas died a year earlier. It had been going on for some time.

An experienced farmer knew when the soil had been leached of nutrients. Seth had spent quite a bit of effort spreading extra manure across Susanna's fields so they would be ready for plowing and planting next spring. At the time, he thought Thomas must have overlooked the basics of agriculture. But now, Seth feared the man had been a derelict farmer. And that didn't set well with Seth.

Had Thomas been a neglectful husband as well? Why had the man been angry and inebriated, then accidentally driven the tractor through the barn wall but not repaired the damage? And did this have something to do with why Susanna seemed a bit offish all the time?

As he took his seat at the kitchen table, Seth shrugged his questions away. It was not his business. And anyway, he had his own problems to cope with. He did not want to get involved with a grieving widow, even if she was talented, hardworking and beautiful. He was Susanna's landlord. She was his daughter's nanny. They helped each other out for the sake of necessity and kindness. Nothing more. There would never be another wife for Seth. He had carried enough heartache with Eve to last a lifetime. Now, he longed for peace and quiet. He did not want to face any more drama by entangling his life with another woman. He had little Miriam and his farm to think of. It was enough. And yet, he could not help wishing for so much more.

Chapter Seven

"Do you want to see the *seinescht*?" Susanna asked.

Wrapped up warm against the bitter wind, she held Miriam against her hip with one arm as she headed toward the pigpen at her farm. Seth was working late in his own fields, so she'd brought the baby home with her this evening. *Mammi* was inside the farmhouse, preparing supper. A nice meat loaf, mashed potatoes and gravy, and steamed vegetables.

As she walked through the barnyard, Susanna carried a bucket filled with slop for the pigs. The frigid breeze fluttered the ties on her white prayer *kapp*. Over the past few weeks, she'd spent her evenings making several little *kapps* for the baby. Since Miriam was almost a year old and now pulling herself up to stand, she'd be walking soon. It was time to get her used to wearing the normal Amish headdress. Just that morning, Susanna had placed one of the tiny *kapps* on the girl's head. At first, Miriam had tugged on the strings and tried to pull the *kapp* off. Susanna had lovingly persisted by distracting the baby and now, Miriam hardly seemed to notice the headwear. That was undoubtedly because the baby frequently wore a warm knit cap, like right now. She would get used to wearing the *kapp* soon enough, too.

"Let's look at the piggies," Susanna said, leaning against the galvanized mesh panels that made up the pigpen.

Setting the bucket on the ground, she held the baby securely as she leaned over the railing to let the girl look inside. The momma sow snorted and came running toward the trough. She knew it was feeding time. Five midsized piglets that had been born six months earlier scurried after their mom, their piercing squeals and grunts filling the evening air.

"Aren't the piggies cute?" Susanna asked the baby.

Miriam babbled happily and clapped her hands together, just as Susanna had taught

her. There was no fear or concern written
across the child's expressive face. She was
so cute that Susanna had to kiss her sweet
cheeks. Susanna couldn't believe how quickly
she'd become used to having the adorable
baby around. Maybe she shouldn't have asked
Seth to find another tender for the little girl.
Susanna wanted Miriam to receive the best
care possible. She had no idea whom Seth
might get to look after his daughter and didn't
like the idea of Miriam being somewhere else.

Setting the baby on her feet in the grass,
Susanna quickly dumped the slop into the
trough and ensured the pigs had plenty of
water. Clutching the side of the railing, Miriam toddled along the fence line in her little
black tights and shoes. She'd soon be walking on her own.

Picking up the child, Susanna retrieved a
metal basket, and went to feed the chickens.
The Amish started teaching their children
farm chores from a very young age. Since
Miriam's mother was gone, Susanna gave
the baby a tiny fist full of chicken feed and
showed her how to toss it on the ground. Miriam gazed at Susanna with sober intensity,
then promptly tried to eat the grain instead.

Susanna laughed and took hold of Miriam's

hand before wiping away pieces of seeds that were sticking to the girl's nose. "*Ne, Liebchen!* This feed isn't for a cute little *boppli*. It's for the chicks. Toss it to them."

To show the child what she meant, Susanna took another handful of grain and flung it on the ground in a sweeping arc. The chickens clucked and gathered around to peck at the earth. Miriam chortled with glee. Susanna gave her a second handful of grain, took hold of her little wrist and helped her toss it aside. Miriam gibbered happily, waving her arms at the squawking birds.

"*Ja*, you like that, don't you? I do, too." Susanna hugged the girl.

While the hens were occupied with eating their supper, Susanna took Miriam inside the dark chicken coop to gather eggs. From the isolation pen, she picked up a medium-sized, fuzzy chick that had been born rather late in the season and let Miriam hold the baby. Miriam immediately squealed with delight and tried to slap the chick with her hand.

"*Ne*, be gentle, *Liebchen*. The chicken is still a *boppli*, just like you," Susanna said.

For emphasis, she took Miriam's hand and brushed it tenderly over the chick's soft, downy feathers.

"See? Like this. Be very gentle. Soft, nice, nice," she spoke in a quiet whisper for emphasis.

Miriam cooed to the chick and proceeded to run her chubby little hand lightly over the bird's tiny body. Susanna was stunned at how quickly Miriam caught on to what she wanted.

"Niss," Miriam said, her quiet voice hissing slightly as she tried to say the word.

Susanna stared in awe. The word was slurred, but Miriam had obviously tried to say "nice." She was so smart, learning to speak more new words every day. Susanna was certain Miriam's speech was quite advanced for a child of her age and she could hardly wait to tell Seth what the baby had said. The girl's sweet voice added such reverence to the moment. And that's when Susanna realized how much she'd come to love this little child. How she wished Thomas had given her a babe before he'd died. How she wished she could be Miriam's mom for real. But Susanna knew that was impossible.

"*Ach*, here you are."

Susanna whirled around and saw Seth's tall shape silhouetted in the open doorway. The afternoon sun glowed behind him, casting his face in shadow.

"Seth!" she cried. "I didn't know you were here. You won't believe what Miriam just said."

She told him about the incident and he smiled as he removed his felt hat and took a step farther into the coop. In the quiet darkness, his presence made Susanna nervous. The only way out was through the door, and he was obstructing her escape.

"Is that right? She is quite a smart little thing." He took another step, reaching toward Miriam to caress the baby's arm.

Susanna swallowed hard. He was standing too close. Blocking her in.

Without warning, a surge of panic gripped her, so fast she couldn't think straight. Her breath caught in her throat and her heart pounded in her chest. Thomas had cornered her in the henhouse once and that dreadful memory raced through her mind like a bolt of lightning. She had to get out of here. Right now.

"Have you milked your cows and goats, yet?" he asked in a pleasant tone, not seeming to notice her duress.

"I… I haven't had time," she said, her voice sounding like a tight squeak.

He reached his other hand toward her and

Susanna hurried past him, carrying Miriam out into the yard. Once she gained her freedom, Susanna relaxed. To avoid him, she headed toward the barn. A quick glance over her shoulder showed the confusion written across Seth's face. As he stepped out of the chicken coop, he stared after her, his eyebrows drawn together, his forehead crinkled in a deep frown.

Having regained her composure, Susanna took several deep breaths to clear her thoughts. She couldn't believe how that dark memory with her husband had surfaced so quickly. But she reminded herself that Seth was not Thomas. She'd been around Miriam's *daed* for some time now. The two men weren't alike in any way at all. And yet, she hadn't been able to stop herself before reacting with fear.

"Susanna, are you *allrecht*?"

She turned and found Seth standing right behind her.

"*Ja*, I... I'm fine," she said.

She stepped back, searching for the disinfectant so she could milk the cows. Miriam squirmed in her arms and began to fuss. Susanna relaxed her tight hold on the baby.

Seth's quizzical expression eased somewhat as he reached for the pitchfork hanging on its hooks on the wall, then drew away.

"Susanna, are you afraid of me?" he asked, standing before her, his big hands seeming to grip the handle of the pitchfork so tightly.

He was so tall. So strong. If he wanted to hurt her, he could. Just like Thomas...

"You're safe with me. Surely you know that," Seth said.

"*Ja*, I know."

"I would never harm you, Susanna. Not ever," he said, his voice filled with conviction.

She believed him. But if they ever married, he could take away her independence. As his wife, she'd be forced to do his bidding. And she couldn't let that happen. Not ever again. It was best to remain single and free.

He stepped away, pitching hay to the horses.

"Susanna! Seth! Supper is ready."

In unison, they turned toward the doorway and saw *Mammi* standing there, wrapped in a warm, black woolen cloak.

"Here! Let me take the *boppli* while you finish your work." *Mammi* reached for the baby, then turned and headed for the door as she called over her shoulder. "As soon as you're finished, *komm* straight into the house so you can eat while it's hot. Don't dawdle around, you two."

Watching her grandmother leave, Susanna was about to call her back. She didn't want to be alone with Seth, or any man, ever again.

Susanna looked at him, filled with suspicion and doubt. He seemed to ignore her as he reached for the three-pegged milking stool. With his back to her, she felt a modicum of ease. And that's when she realized how foolish she must seem. How insecure and silly. And yet, she couldn't help feeling full of misgivings. She was drawn to this man, she couldn't deny it. She tried to tell herself it was because he'd been so kind to her and he was Miriam's *vadder*. But deep inside, she knew it was something more. Something she didn't understand.

"I… I'll finish gathering the eggs," she said.

He gave a nod but didn't look at her. "*Gut!* Then, you should go on into the house. I'll finish up here and bring the milk in shortly."

She hesitated. It wasn't an order, just a respectful suggestion. He kept working and she stepped away. He was strong and competent, yet he never tried to wield his masculine power over her the way Thomas had done.

But if she dropped her guard and let Seth get too close, he might break her heart the way her husband had done. And she couldn't take that chance. Never again.

She stepped out into the cool evening air. After gathering the eggs, she hurried to the house and stepped inside the kitchen. The bright lights and warm aroma of food surrounded her. As she removed her coat and scarf and hung them on a hook by the door, she couldn't believe how kind Seth was toward her. Surely he didn't know what she'd gone through with Thomas, yet he was always compassionate and thoughtful.

After they'd married, Thomas had never been sensitive to her needs. He'd never acknowledged her wishes or ever treated her like a valued wife. He'd dominated her with cruel, brute force. If she wanted to do something, he refused to allow it. She'd soon learned to use reverse psychology on him, which helped a little bit. She could only imagine what he would say if he found out she was running her own noodle business. He never would have agreed to letting her open her own store. Yet, Seth had allowed her the use of his building and stayed out of her affairs. And the way he gave her free rein with

Miriam, it was almost as if he had complete faith in her. He trusted her judgment, something she'd never had from Thomas.

"Is Seth coming in?" *Mammi* asked from where she stood in front of the stove.

Miriam sat in her high chair, gumming a crust of bread.

Susanna nodded. "*Ja*, he'll be here soon."

As she cleaned the eggs and put them in the gas-powered fridge to chill, she couldn't help comparing Seth with her husband. Without being asked, Seth had done so much work on her farm already. He was so gentle with Miriam. So quiet and considerate. He always appeared so helpful. Perhaps he wasn't like Thomas at all. Maybe her husband had been an anomaly and other women enjoyed a happy marriage with their spouses. It was something to think about.

What on earth had gotten into Susanna? Seth couldn't understand her actions. When he'd stepped into the chicken coop, her eyes had widened with absolute terror. It was as if she thought he was going to throttle her. She'd rushed past him so fast that he'd had to catch himself before he was knocked flat. If he didn't know better, he'd think she was frightened. Of him. And that didn't make sense. Not once since he'd known her had he ever lifted a hand toward her, little Miriam or even one of their livestock. If nothing else, he was a kind man. He didn't have much temper, which was probably why he'd tolerated Eve's antics better than most men would have done. But that didn't explain Susanna's actions today. She'd never behaved like that before and he sensed it had something specific to do with the henhouse.

He hung the pitchfork back on its hooks on the wall, then reached for a metal bucket. Placing several scoops of grain inside, he offered it to Billy and Luna, Susanna's two Percheron draft horses. As each large animal ate its fair share, Seth rubbed their necks, then went to check the water trough before he milked the cows. The chores didn't take long. He'd done them a trillion times before and knew what to do.

As he worked, he realized Susanna didn't have much livestock. With her twenty acres, her farm had the potential to become a small but fine place. It was a shame that Thomas had let it fall into disrepair. And then a thought occurred to Seth. Had Thomas been harsh with Susanna? Surely not. Word traveled quickly among the Amish. The gossip mill churned nonstop. If Thomas was abusing his wife, everyone would have heard about it.

Unless Susanna had kept it to herself.

Hmm. So, what was going on here? Seth wasn't sure and didn't know if it was his place to ask. After all, she wasn't his kinsman or spouse and it wasn't really his business.

As he tended the two cows and goats, the whooshing sounds of milk hitting the clean buckets soothed his jangled nerves. Outside, he could hear the wind picking up and lashing against the trees and rooftop. All was warm and comfortable inside the barn as the livestock ate their supper and settled for the night. The calm gave Seth time to think.

Susanna was such a hard worker. With her mild manners and generous heart, he couldn't imagine ever lifting a hand in violence toward her. Occasionally, he'd heard that some Amish men mistreated their wives, children and livestock. Not Seth. The thought of hitting or whipping another person or animal was alien to him. And it wasn't something the Lord would condone, either. Even as crazy as Eve had acted sometimes, he had never been tempted to strike her. Not even once. Never had he tried to dominate her in any way. Instead, he'd used loving persuasion, hoping she would listen and choose to change her ways of her own accord. If only she had shown some humility and expressed a desire to return to church, the shunning would have been removed. He would have even forgiven her indiscretions with other men. He wasn't perfect by any stretch of the imagination, but he tried every day to follow the admonition of Jesus Christ to love others as he loved himself.

Shaking his head, he put all the tools away, then carried the pails of milk outside and secured the barn door for the night. As he crossed the yard, the sun was just tucking behind the mountains to the west. Heavy clouds filled the heavens above. Dark shadows played across the fields to the south. The warm glow of lights shimmered from the windows of the farmhouse and he caught the scrumptious aroma of something good cooking for supper. Susanna and her grandmother didn't need to be told what to do, either. No force was needed to get them to work hard and serve others. How he wished Eve had been half as diligent as Susanna was.

As he stepped up onto the back porch, the kitchen door opened wide for him.

"It's freezing cold out here. *Komm* inside

and have your supper." *Mammi* welcomed him with a wide smile as she reached to take one of the pails of milk.

As he set the other bucket on the sideboard, he whisked his hat off his head and placed it on a hook by the door.

"*Ach*, something smells *gut*," he said, tossing a hesitant smile toward Susanna.

She stood before the counter, slicing a loaf of homemade bread. She didn't look at him and he hoped he hadn't offended her in any way. Once again, his mind sorted through every encounter he could remember having with her, trying to think if he'd done something to earn her enmity. But he came up with nothing. No logical reason why she should be frightened of him when they were standing inside the henhouse. And then, he thought perhaps he'd imagined it all.

"Da-da-da," Miriam called from her high chair as she kicked her little legs.

Correction. It was Susanna's high chair. And for some crazy reason, Seth felt at home in this house. As if he and Miriam actually belonged here. An odd thought, surely.

"Sit down and we'll eat," *Mammi* urged.

Since he'd already washed good before milking the cows, he took a seat closest to

Miriam. The baby laughed and he reached out to caress her smooth cheek.

"*Hallo*, sweetums. Did you have a *gut* day?" he asked.

Miriam gabbled a bunch of nonsense in response and he had to laugh.

"She's getting to be quite vocal, isn't she?" he asked no one in particular.

"*Ja*, she learned another new word today. She said *yum*," Susanna supplied, her voice rather cheerful.

Seth looked at Susanna, delighted that everything seemed to have returned to normal. He hated the thought of having animosity between himself and this kind woman. For some reason, he felt as though they should be close friends. But that wasn't possible. They had a business relationship, nothing more. What he needed right now was peace and stability, not complications in his personal life. And yet…

"Is that right?" he said, gazing at his daughter.

"*Ja*, she jabbers all the time. She must be quite a smart little thing," Dorothy said. "But you'll be sorry she's speaking so much in a year or two."

He tilted his head in curiosity. "And why is that?"

Dorothy chuckled. "If she's anything like most little girls, you won't be able to shut her up."

They all laughed and it broke the tension in the air.

After blessing the food, they tucked into their meal. Somewhere outside, Seth heard the lowing of contented cattle. Darkness had fallen and the warmth of home and companionship settled over the room. He hated the thought of taking Miriam outside into the cold for the short drive to their home.

"You and Miriam will have Thanksgiving dinner with us, won't you?" Dorothy asked.

Susanna's head jerked up and he could tell her grandmother hadn't asked her permission before inviting him.

"Um, are you sure that's not too much of an imposition?" he asked.

"Of course not," Dorothy laughed. "I've seen what's inside your fridge. I don't expect you'll do well if you have to roast your own turkey and mash some potatoes."

He chuckled. "You're probably right. I'm not much of a cook."

What she said was true but he wondered if Susanna wanted him here. He waited, seeking some sign of approval from her.

"We'll have plenty of food. You should take your meal here with us," Susanna finally said.

He caught the genuine inflection in her voice and knew she meant it. And yet, it seemed as if she was fighting against herself.

"We'd like that very much," he said, glancing at Miriam.

"It's settled, then. It'll be like the old days when I had lots of *familye* around. Lots of fun and laughter." Dorothy smiled with pleasure, as if she were lost in her fond memories.

As they chatted about their day's work, Seth noticed Susanna was rather quiet. But even then, he couldn't help feeling like he belonged here. For the first time in his life, he felt like he had people who needed him. People depending on him. Like a real *familye*.

After supper, he helped clear the table. He knew most men disappeared into the living room, to read, relax or repair bridles or other equipment. But with Eve being gone so much, Seth had learned to wash dishes, even if he did let them pile up sometimes.

Standing next to the sink, he picked up a dish towel and dried a plate while Susanna washed. She glanced at him, her expression filled with misgivings. Her amber eyes held a sadness and he longed to make her smile. A chestnut curl had come loose from her prayer *kapp* and he almost reached up to tuck it back behind her ear.

Almost.

"Did you have many customers in the store today?" he asked instead.

She kept her head bowed over the sink as the soapy suds swirled around her slender hands.

"*Ja*, the rush doesn't seem to be wearing off. The customers love my weekly specials. I've noticed a lot of repeat shoppers," she said, her voice almost too quiet.

"*Gut!* I hope it stays that way. You've done a great job setting everything up. You should be pleased with yourself." He paused a moment, wondering what he could say to help her relax around him. "I spoke to Ruth Lapp this morning. She was in the general store when I popped in for some ice melt."

"Oh?" she said, still not looking at him.

"She said she'd be happy to start looking after Miriam for me in January, once the holidays are over with."

Susanna jerked her head up and stared at him. "Really? So soon?"

He nodded and reached to take a large pan from her as she rinsed it off. Their fingers brushed together briefly and she yanked her hand away fast.

"It's not really so soon," he said, pretending indifference as he dried the pan and set it aside. "It's less than a couple of months away. Can you continue to look after Miriam until then? I know you're awfully busy at the shop."

"Of course. Whatever Miriam needs. Once Ruth starts tending Miriam, I'll start paying you rent for the store." She pulled the plug in the sink and let the water swirl down the drain.

Wringing out the dishrag, she turned and busied herself with wiping down the counters and stove. With her back to him, he couldn't be certain, but he got the impression she was upset again. Was it because he was standing so close, or because he'd told her Miriam would be leaving right after Christmas?

After shrugging into his warm winter coat, he went into the living room and picked up his sleeping daughter. Dorothy was slumped in a chair nearby, her soft snores filling the air.

After pulling a knit cap over Miriam's white *kapp*, he tucked a warm blanket around her little body to shield her from the cold night air. As he stepped outside, Susanna followed from a safe distance.

"*Danke* for your help tonight," she said.

"And *danke* to you, too. I'll see you in the morning," he said.

With her arms folded against the chilling breeze, she accompanied him to his buggy and waited while he settled the baby in her safety seat and was ready to leave.

"*Mach's gut,*" Susanna bid farewell as she lifted a hand and stepped back from the buggy.

"*Gut nacht,*" he returned with a nod.

With nothing left to say, he switched on the single battery-operated headlight he'd affixed to the front of his buggy, took the leather lead lines into his hands and slapped them lightly against his road horse's back. The carriage jostled slightly as it pulled forward.

When he reached the end of the lane leading to the county road, he glanced in his rearview mirror. Susanna had gone inside and he felt a lonely hollowness deep in his chest. He thought he was the only one with a broken heart. But maybe Susanna had her own sadness to deal with. Maybe Thomas hadn't been a good husband to her after all. And that upset Seth, though he didn't understand why. Susanna wasn't his concern. She wasn't his wife. She and her kind grandmother weren't his *familye*. No, not at all. But they needed each other right now. They all deserved to be happy.

Beginning January 1, he'd take Miriam over to Ruth Lapp's house for childcare. Ruth lived only a couple miles away, so it should work okay. Apparently she'd decided she could use some extra income and agreed to tend Miriam. He wouldn't see Susanna again, except occasionally for her to pay rent on her store or at church on Sundays. That suited Seth fine. Because his heart had been broken once before. He would never become involved in another woman's life again. It was best this way. For both him and Miriam. He had to protect his little one's heart as much as his own. It would be best for Susanna, too. Or at least, that's what he told himself.

Chapter Eight

As the last customer of the day left the store, Susanna flipped the Closed sign around in the window and locked the front door. She'd set the hours for her shop to close at five o'clock. But when shoppers kept coming in, she wasn't about to shoo them away. So, she'd kept waiting on them while Mammi worked in the back rooms. Their diligence seemed to be paying off. In her wildest dreams, Susanna had never expected this much business.

A clock buzzed in the kitchen and she hurried toward it. Perfect timing. The batch of pumpkin bread *Mammi* had slid into the oven an hour earlier was done. If Seth would come inside and eat his supper, she could clean up and go home.

Switching off the light to the salesroom, Susanna retrieved her mitts and pulled the oven door open. A blast of fragrant heat struck her in the face and she ducked her head. The aroma of cinnamon, nutmeg and allspice wafted through the air. The entire store smelled like the holidays. One customer had caught the yummy smell and even asked if Susanna sold her bread. She thought about speaking with *Mammi* to see if they wanted to expand their noodles into homemade bread, too. Maybe they could make it just for the holidays. They'd have to buy a second oven and perhaps a gas-powered freezer. It was something to consider.

Lifting the four bread pans onto cooling racks she'd laid out on the counter, she noticed the full, moist loaves had baked to perfection. As she inserted a toothpick into a couple of them and withdrew it to ensure the batter was done in the middle, she glanced at the clock on the wall. A quarter past seven. They'd all been working long hours.

Hurrying back to the salesroom, she emptied the till into a cash box. She'd take it home with her and count out the receipts from there. Making some notes on her inventory list, she realized she needed to make noodles again. Maybe she could work on that tomorrow, while *Mammi* minded the store.

Returning to the kitchen, she gazed out the

window. It was dark but she caught a flash of movement from the barn. Seth was headed this way, packing two shiny metal buckets, which she knew carried fresh milk.

She peered at the doorway leading to the apartment overhead, hoping to see *Mammi* there. The elderly woman had taken the baby upstairs a few minutes earlier, to get the child bathed and ready for bed. Susanna knew it would be another half hour before her grandmother came back down stairs and she hated to be alone with Seth in the meantime. But it couldn't be helped.

She sighed, hearing the back door open, then the sounds of his thudding boots as he stepped inside. Within moments, he appeared in the kitchen and set the buckets of milk on the counter near the fridge. She'd trained him not to go tromping upstairs where he might wake the baby. He'd complied easily, seeming as patient and kind as the day was long.

"Whew! It's bitter cold out there. I think we might get a dusting of snow tonight," he exclaimed as he doffed his black felt hat, gloves and coat and hung them on hooks by the outer door.

His cheeks and nose were pink from the frigid air. As he came into the warm light, he smiled, looking more handsome than a man had a right to be.

She forced herself to look away.

"Sit down," she said, speaking rather brusquely. "*Mammi* and I have already eaten. I'd better get you fed so we can get on the road to home. I don't want to be caught in a snowstorm."

"*Ne*, of course not. I'm sorry to keep you out so late tonight."

He sounded so apologetic as he pulled out a chair and she immediately regretted being so terse with him.

"You didn't make us late. I just barely locked the front door."

His eyebrows lifted in expectation as he sat before the table. "You were busy again today?"

She knew he was talking about the store and nodded. "*Ja*, it hasn't seemed to let up one bit."

"You're a *gut* businesswoman, Susanna. I'm happy for you."

His words of praise brought a flush of pleasure to her chest. For some reason, his regard meant a lot to her, though she didn't understand why.

He gazed at the counter next to the sink. Sixteen quart jars filled with pretty applesauce sat cooling on an old, tattered towel along with eight quarts of sliced apples…the last of the golden delicious apples *Mammi* had bottled for him earlier that morning. Standing along the wall next to the fridge, several drying racks were filled with noodles they'd made the day before. Tomorrow, she and *Mammi* would package and label them and add them to the shelves in the outer room. And none too soon. With so much business, they'd had to increase their production of pasta to keep up with the demand. But Susanna didn't mind. After the holidays, she would visit stores in neighboring towns to see if they would be willing to carry her noodles. She had it all planned out. She'd take samples and flyers with her and set a reasonable wholesale price. Once the orders started coming in, she could simply ship the noodles to those stores via the post office. She'd hire one or two teenaged Amish girls to help with the work. Hopefully, she could get a couple of lucrative contracts and would start shipping her products immediately afterward.

"It looks like you've been busy. I'm sorry to keep you so late," Seth said again.

"Don't be silly. The work has to be done." She didn't look at him as she reached for a bowl and filled it with hearty beef stew from a pot she'd left simmering on the stove.

After sliding it onto the table in front of him, she retrieved a plate and laid several thick slices of corn bread on it. Without a word, she bowed her head as he blessed the food. While he ate, she released the pumpkin bread from their pans so the loaves could cool, then filled the sink with hot, sudsy water to wash the dishes. As soon as Seth had eaten his fill, she'd take *Mammi* home to the chores awaiting them there. A while earlier, Susanna had seen the tired slump of *Mammi's* shoulders. She'd send the elderly woman up to bed while she went outside to feed the pigs and other animals. It wouldn't take long and she'd get the chores done fast. Then, she also could rest.

As if reading her mind, Seth paused in his eating to look up. "I went over to your place an hour ago and fed your livestock. I milked your cows and goats, too, and put the milk in the well house. You'll want to separate the cream in the morning but there shouldn't be much work for you to do there."

She stilled, listening to his voice. Though she kept her face averted, she was highly conscious of him. "That was kind of you but you don't need to do those things."

"*Ja*, I do. You've been frantically busy here at

the store. People are coming and going in a constant stream. When would you find the time?"

Feeling irritated by his words, she set a wooden bowl on the counter with an overly hard thump. He had a point but she didn't like him doing things at her farm without asking her first. If she became too beholden to him, he might think he owned her. That he could boss her around. She didn't like the thought of losing control over her own life.

"I'd stay up late until it's done, if that's what it took. I'm an independent woman and perfectly capable of doing it all by myself," she snapped.

He stared at her, his eyes crinkled in a quizzical expression. "I know that, Susanna. I would never question your abilities. I was just trying to help."

Oh, that made her feel even worse. Of course he was trying to help. She wished Thomas had been half as considerate. But because of her husband, she didn't trust easily. She'd learned the hard way to never let down her guard with a man. But Seth wasn't making things easy for her. And yet, he made everything easier. And she couldn't accept that. Not if it meant she might have to relinquish her independence.

Oh, dear! She was so confused right now.

"Is Dorothy upstairs with Miriam?" he asked, his voice soft and conciliatory.

She nodded, not daring to speak. She rinsed several plates and bowls before placing them in the dish drain.

"The *boppli* has eaten and had her evening bath," she finally said. "She was plumb tuckered out. She'll probably sleep through the night for you."

He grunted. "*Gut!* You've got her well trained, Susanna. She hardly wakes up at all anymore. She seems much happier and relaxed since you started looking after her. I think having a regular routine has helped get her on a set schedule."

Susanna chuckled. "With three adults tending to her every need, I'm not surprised. She's so sweet, it's hard to keep my hands off her. And all the customers love her, too. I don't dare take my eyes off her for fear someone might steal her away. So, I just carry her with me all over the store, unless *Mammi* has a free moment to tend her."

He laughed and lifted his empty bowl for a refill. "You've got that right. I feel good knowing she's in such *gut* hands. May I have seconds, please?"

She nodded, took his bowl and filled it to the brim before setting it on the table again. He dug in, eating hungrily. And watching him, she couldn't help feeling like an old married couple chatting about their daily activities while their baby slept peacefully upstairs. Except they weren't a couple and they never would be. She couldn't allow that to happen. Not ever again!

"Miriam looks so much like her *mudder*," Susanna said. "Sometimes I wonder what physical traits she might have acquired from you."

He didn't respond immediately and she glanced his way. He held his spoon aloft as he stared at her, an odd look of consternation on his face. Then, he set his spoon aside and picked up a piece of bread, though he didn't take a bite.

"You're right, of course. She looks nothing like me. But maybe that's a *gut* thing," he finally said.

Susanna tilted her head to the side. Had she caught a note of remorse in his voice? Surely she imagined it. But then again, maybe she'd hurt his feelings with her musings. After all, Seth was Miriam's daddy. It couldn't feel nice to be told that she looked nothing like him.

"Who knows? Children change as they grow older. Maybe Miriam will become tall like you. Or maybe her blond curls will darken to the color of damp sand, like your hair. Perhaps Miriam has your personality instead of Eve's. She's very smart and observant, not that Eve wasn't those things. But I've never met a *boppli* who appears more easygoing than your *dochder*," she said.

She didn't add that the thought of watching Miriam grow into a lovely, fine woman filled Susanna with anticipation. She wanted to be here with Seth to see that happen. And that thought scared her to death because it meant she would be near Seth for years to come. And she couldn't do that. Could she?

He looked up, a tight smile curving his lips. "I'm glad to hear you think I'm smart."

Reaching for a towel, she dried more dishes. "Of course you're smart. Look at everything you've accomplished here on your farm. It all runs quite smoothly. And my place has never looked better, either. That's all thanks to you. I am grateful, Seth. I… I hope you understand."

He nodded and tucked into his second serving of stew. When he finished, he looked at the pumpkin bread. "Is that for us to eat? Or did you make it for someone else?"

"Both. *Mammi* made it. Over the holidays,

we usually give away lots of pumpkin bread to our friends. But we eat whatever we want, too. Pumpkin is highly nutritious."

Letting go of her misgivings, she reached for a knife and sliced off two thick pieces of warm bread for him. After all, she didn't want contention with this man. Thomas's violent tendencies weren't Seth's fault. She had to remember that.

He bit into the bread and chewed for several seconds, making yummy sounds in the back of his throat. "This is delicious. So moist and sweet. It's more like a cake. I haven't eaten pumpkin bread in years."

"Really? Didn't Eve make pumpkin bread for you? I know she was an excellent cook."

He shook his head, took another bite, then closed his eyes as he chewed slowly. "*Ne*, I tried to get her to bake and cook, but she didn't want to. She was *gut* at it but lost interest in everything except…"

Except the drugs. He didn't have to say it for Susanna to know his thoughts.

How sad. The more Susanna learned about Eve, the more she realized Seth had been trapped in a difficult marriage he couldn't change. Just like Susanna. And though she felt sorry for him, she wasn't willing to become his surrogate wife. Beginning January 1, Miriam would go over to Ruth Lapp's house for childcare each day. Susanna would hire a driver to take her to the neighboring towns where she would peddle her pasta to the general stores there. She was a businesswoman. She had a life of her own. And it didn't include Seth and Miriam on a long-term basis. She was determined and focused. She wasn't about to let a kind widower and his sweet daughter change any of her goals.

"When I first married Eve, she said she'd like to start a bakery here in the store." The moment Seth said the words, he regretted them. Thinking about his wife only made him sad.

"Why didn't she do it?" Susanna asked.

He shrugged, watching her pour the remaining stew from the pan into a glass bowl. After covering the leftovers, she stowed them in the fridge. Seth figured that would be their lunch tomorrow afternoon.

"She couldn't seem to think about anything but drugs," he said. "She was obsessed. When she was here at *heemet*, she was like a caged tiger, nervous and wanting to leave. I couldn't seem to help her. I tried to take her to a professional doctor at the hospital in town for help but she refused. I didn't know what to do. On church Sundays, she would go into people's bathrooms and steal pills from their medicine cabinets. Once, she even stole phencyclidine from a veterinary business in town."

Susanna's mouth dropped open in surprise and she looked at him from over her shoulder. "Phencyclidine?"

He nodded. "You might have heard it called PCP. It's a horse tranquilizer."

"*Ja*, I've heard of PCP before. But I can't imagine a person taking such a strong drug."

He snorted. "Me, neither. Whenever Eve got into trouble with the law, I bailed her out of jail. But the last time it happened, I warned her I wouldn't do it again. That was before she came *heemet* to have Miriam. And you know the rest of the story…"

Susanna made a sympathetic sound in the back of her throat and he looked up.

"You've been through a lot and I'm sorry," she said.

Her forehead was creased, her eyes filled with shock, sympathy and pity. And seeing her like this, he immediately regretted confiding in her. In his need to speak about it, he'd let down his guard. Susanna was so easy to talk to. But if he wasn't careful, he might accidentally slip up and tell her that Miriam wasn't his biological daughter. And that could be disastrous.

Setting his fork aside, he scooted back his chair. "Supper was delicious. *Danke* for a great meal. Now, I'd better get upstairs and relieve Dorothy. It's time the two of you were on the road to *heemet*."

She ducked her head and returned to the sink. She looked so small and vulnerable standing there. A protective surge rose up within him. For just a moment, he longed to see her smile and hear her laugh again. To say something that would make her feel good. But doing so might give her the wrong idea. And he couldn't do that.

"You're *willkomm*," she said.

As he stood, he looked at her to see if she might say something more. There were so many things he longed to tell her. So many thoughts he wished he could share with someone who cared about him and Miriam. But he knew this wasn't the time and Susanna wasn't that person.

He was alone now, with no one to love except his little girl. He thought he'd accepted that. He was a strong, capable man and didn't need a woman in his life. Did he? Not after what he'd gone through with Eve. But then, there were times like right now, when he became a little bit too introspective and his feelings slipped out without him intending them to. Fatigue, a warm kitchen and a delicious meal had that effect on him. He'd become too relaxed around Susanna and her kindhearted grandmother. And that must stop right now. Because they weren't his *familye*. He wasn't responsible for them, nor could he keep them. Not ever again. After Christmas, Ruth Lapp would be tending Miriam and he wouldn't be eating his meals here in this kitchen anymore.

"I think I'll go up now. I've got to process my milk." He reached for the two buckets he'd left sitting on the counter.

She didn't look around or acknowledge him and he couldn't help wondering if she wished he'd go away. And then, a thought occurred to him. What had Thomas done that had made her become so determined to remain free and independent of another man?

Hmm. That was an odd idea. Surely Thomas hadn't done anything to make Susanna shun men. Or had he?

"*Ja*, if you'll send *Mammi* down, I'll take her *heemet*," she said.

"*Gut nacht*, then," he said.

She didn't respond. She barely acknowledged him.

As he stepped into the hallway and mounted the stairs leading to his lonely apartment above, he couldn't help feeling suddenly empty inside and so very desolate. He told himself that life would get easier. Time would pass and Miriam would grow. The years would march on. And yet, he couldn't help thinking he was a neutral bystander and the world was passing him by. Joy had fled him. His hope in the future now failed. He couldn't seem to get it back. Couldn't imagine anything worthwhile to live for, except Miriam. The trauma he'd experienced with Eve had run its course. He'd experienced enough drama to last a lifetime. The thought of marrying someone else made his veins flood with anxiety. How could he ever trust another woman? What if he got hurt again? He couldn't stand that pain a second time. And he had to protect Miriam, too.

Maybe Susanna felt the same way. They were two forlorn people who didn't want or need love in their lives. And yet, a niggling doubt told him that wasn't true. But one thing was certain. He was determined never to open his heart and divulge personal information to Susanna again. If the secret he kept ever got out, it could cost him everything.

Chapter Nine

~⚬~

The week before Thanksgiving, Susanna stood beside the cash register in her store. Sunlight gleamed through the wide picture windows she'd just finished cleaning. They'd had a light dusting of snow the night before. With the gray clouds filling the sky, she wanted the chore finished before it snowed again in earnest later tonight.

Now, she tallied her inventory list one last time. Hmm. She'd better order more alfredo sauce. And red sauce, too. Next to the noodles, they seemed to be her biggest sellers. And she'd better make more spaghetti tomorrow or she'd run out next week. She planned to close the store on Thursday for Thanksgiving. Other than helping *Mammi* prepare a lovely feast, she was planning to take the day off. But Black Friday, she hoped to do a lot of business and that the holiday shoppers flocked her way.

Keeping the shelves stocked with inventory had become a bit difficult but she and *Mammi* had met the challenge, so far. It had been a busy morning and she was alone. *Mammi* was upstairs putting Miriam down for a nap.

She jotted a couple of more notes to herself. The bell over the front door tinkled gaily, heralding another customer. Looking up, she saw a young *Englisch* man step inside. He appeared professional, dressed in a pair of pressed blue dress slacks. His fine, woolen coat was unbuttoned, showing his starched white shirt and tie underneath. His shiny black shoes were immaculate, not a single smudge on them.

Slipping her inventory list into a drawer, she pasted a smile on her face and stepped around the counter to greet him.

"Hello. What can I help you with?" she asked, speaking perfect English.

He didn't smile but glanced around the room, as if he were searching for someone. That's when she noticed he held a white envelope in his hand.

"Is Seth Lehman here?" he asked in a no-nonsense voice.

Obviously, he wasn't interested in pasta.

But his efficient manner gave her a bad feeling. Without asking, she sensed something was wrong.

She nodded. "Yes, I believe he's in the kitchen eating his lunch."

"Would you mind getting him for me, please?" the man asked.

"Of course." Turning, she headed that way, feeling puzzled. She realized she should have asked who he was.

The man followed her but stopped just in front of the counter. Hurrying into the kitchen, Susanna found Seth sitting at the table, wolfing down a bowl of *Mammi's* homemade chicken-corn soup. His black felt hat and warm winter coat rested on a peg by the back door. As usual, he'd worked hard that morning, spreading manure across his fallow fields before plowing it in to the rich, dark soil. Yesterday, he'd replaced the broken blades on his hay mower so it would be ready for harvesting in late spring. Susanna knew he planned to repeat these same chores at her place later that afternoon. He was busy, taking meticulous care of both their farms.

"Seth?" she called, feeling oddly pleased to see him in spite of her desire to remain aloof.

He turned, holding his spoon in midair as

he chewed. His eyes glimmered with recognition and his mouth curved slightly. Almost a smile, but not quite. He seemed to catch himself and looked away.

"What is it?" he asked, taking a bite of bread and butter.

"There's a man here to see you," she said, indicating the front of the store.

Swallowing, he set the spoon down, wiped the corner of his mouth with the back of his hand and stood.

"Who is it?" he asked as he stepped over to the door. His forehead crinkled with curiosity.

She hurried out of his way, opening a path to the hall. "I don't know. But he looks rather official."

Seth frowned as he headed out into the store. She followed, feeling more than intrigued.

"Are you looking for me?" Seth greeted the stranger.

The young man tilted his head to one side. "Are you Seth Lehman?"

"Yes, I am Seth," he said.

The man handed the envelope to him. "This is for you, sir."

Sir! The *Englisch* rarely spoke with such respect. What was going on?

Seth took the packet and turned it over, his

eyes crinkled in confusion. His name was scrawled across the front of the envelope. "What is this?"

"You have been served, sir."

Without another word, the young man turned and walked purposefully out the front door. For a moment, Seth stared after the guy, looking a bit stunned and dismayed. Then, he ran his finger beneath the sealed flap, opened the envelope and removed the pages.

While he read the enclosed documents, Susanna stood there in silence and waited. Seth licked his upper lip and read through the contents a second time. Finally, he released a heavy sigh of disbelief and shook his head, muttering beneath his breath.

"*Ne*, it can't be true."

She barely caught his words. From his expression, she could tell he was more than upset. His hand dropped to his side, his fingers barely clinging to the papers as he closed his eyes and lowered his chin to his chest for several long seconds. It was as if he were in pain and needed to absorb the impact for a moment.

"Seth, what is it?" Susanna stepped closer, not knowing how to comfort him.

He lifted his head and looked at her, his eyes filled with misery, his face pale with disbelief.

"It's my greatest fear in this life come true. I thought I'd faced the worst when I buried my wife, but it's not over with, yet," he said.

What did he mean? That didn't make sense.

"I don't see how I can keep word of it from getting out now. So, you might as well hear it from me," he murmured.

He held the front page up for her to see and she quickly read the words at the top. *Petition for Change of Child Custody.*

She met his gaze. "What… What is that? What does it mean?"

"It means a man named Robert Thompson is claiming he is Miriam's biological *vadder*," he said. "He's filed an expedited petition for a *change of custody of a minor*. I've been ordered to appear before a circuit judge in the courtroom here in Riverton next Tuesday morning at eight o'clock."

Susanna gasped. "Tuesday! But that's so soon. It's right before Thanksgiving."

He lifted one shoulder, as if he didn't understand it, either. "The petition says it's been expedited. I'm guessing because it involves a child, they want to hurry up the process."

"But how can this be? Miriam's your *boppli*. You're her *daed*. I don't understand."

Seth set the papers next to the cash register, then braced both of his hands against the counter and lowered his head, as if to keep himself from falling down. He looked so forlorn standing there. So alone.

She touched his shoulder. "Seth, are you *allrecht*? Do you need to sit down?"

He shook his head. "*Ne*, I… I need…"

He didn't finish his thought and she realized he didn't know what he needed right then.

"It's not right. You're Miriam's *vadder*. This couldn't be true, Seth. Could it?" she asked.

He looked at her, his hazel eyes filled with fear and doubt. "I… I'm afraid it could very well be true. For some time, I've feared I wasn't Miriam's true *vadder*. Eve claimed I was and I'm on the birth certificate, but the dates never lined up right. Still, in my heart, I'll always be Miriam's *daedi*."

Oh, no. In a rush, Susanna understood the implications. Eve had been shunned for adultery but it never occurred to Susanna that Seth might not be Miriam's father. She pressed a hand over her mouth, feeling stunned.

"I just never thought this would come to light in such a public manner," Seth said. "When Eve came home and said she was expecting a *boppli*, she mentioned a man named

Rob. He gave her the drugs she was taking. He was also her…handler."

Susanna didn't understand. "Handler?"

"He sent her to other men to sell drugs and pay her for services."

Services? Susanna dropped her mouth open in absolute shock. She could just imagine what all that entailed and it wasn't good. And the thought of Miriam living in such a sordid world made Susanna recoil with outrage.

"*Ne!* It's too horrible to consider," she said.

"*Ja*, you're right. Eve told me she'd been staying with this man named Rob for a couple of months. I'm guessing he's the one who has filed the paternity suit," Seth said.

Susanna's mind whirled. Seth was not Miriam's daddy? The thought was too awful, too monstrous to consider. And yet, here it was. Right smack in front of them. Seth had been ordered to appear before a judge. There was no way around it. The Amish hated being under the control of *Englisch* law but they had to live in this society. They didn't want trouble.

"Will they try to take Miriam away from you?" Susanna asked, her heart sick with the thought of losing such a dear, sweet baby to someone who didn't even know her.

Seth met her gaze. His eyes glistened with

moisture and she thought finally, this strong man might break down and cry.

"They might. If they can prove Miriam isn't mine, they could take her from me," he said, his voice a hoarse whisper.

"Oh, *ne!*" she cried.

The ramifications of Eve's thoughtless actions came into sharp focus. Seth could lose his daughter. Susanna didn't know who this Rob person was but she was almost certain he was *Englisch*. And if he was truly Miriam's father, Susanna had no doubt he would pull the girl into a world that wasn't good for any child to be living in. How could any judge allow an innocent baby to be placed in such a home? It was unthinkable. To take Miriam and give her to a man who didn't know and love her, it was unreal. Surely no thinking human being would agree to such a thing. And Susanna realized that, just because a person could have a baby, it didn't mean they should be parents and that they would take good care of that child.

An urgency built within her and she understood Seth's anxiousness only too well. She voiced her thoughts out loud, desperate for him to do something to stop this tragedy from happening.

"Believe me, I'm heartsick by the possibility of losing my *boppli*, too," he said.

"Think what would happen to Miriam if she was raised by such a man. You've got to fight it, Seth."

"I intend to. But first, I've got to pay a visit to Bishop Yoder. Will you accompany me, Susanna? I... I need some clarity. Someone else's perspective. And you're about the only person I can trust right now."

She blinked in surprise. He trusted her? How could that be? After everything he'd been through with Eve, he had as much reason to distrust her as she had to distrust him. But his declaration softened something inside her. If he could trust her, maybe she could trust him, too. Maybe they weren't so far apart in the world as she first thought. It was more to think about.

He wanted her to go with him. Against her will, she was being drawn into his troubles. But maybe that had already happened the day she'd agreed to provide childcare for Miriam. Susanna loved Seth's baby. Very much. And because she cared about Miriam, she cared about Seth, too. Whether she liked it or not, she was neck-deep involved in their welfare.

She took a deep inhale of resignation and

released it. "Give me a moment to tell *Mammi* where I'm going. She can mind the store and look after Miriam while I'm gone."

She turned toward the stairs leading up to his apartment.

"I'll get the buggy ready and meet you out front," he called after her.

As she walked upstairs, she gripped the handrail so hard that her knuckles whitened. This wasn't really happening. Was it? And yet, Seth confirmed it could be true. He might not be Miriam's father.

Susanna had tried so hard to remain distant from Seth and his sweet little girl. But now, her heart was breaking at the thought of losing Miriam. She longed to tell Seth to settle his own affairs. That she didn't want to be drawn into this debacle. After everything she'd gone through with Thomas, she didn't need any more drama in her life. And yet, what kind of daughter of *Gott* would she be if she turned her back on Seth and Miriam now? They needed her help, whether she was prepared to offer it or not. Yes, she had a choice. She could refuse to go with Seth. Refuse to be any kind of support in his time of need...

No! She couldn't do that. Turning her back on him went against everything she believed in. Her love for *Gott* and belief in service to others wouldn't allow her to walk away. But as she went into the apartment and told *Mammi* what was going on, she felt as though she were drowning. *Mammi* was understandably upset, too. Together, they silently stood in Miriam's bedroom and gazed down at the baby. Such a beautiful, sleeping child. She looked so innocent. So sweet and precious, with no idea her future was in grave jeopardy.

Back in the living room, Susanna gripped her grandmother's hands as the truth of this baby's predicament washed over her in horrifying waves. To help alleviate their fears, the two women took a few minutes to kneel in front of the sofa where Susanna uttered a quick prayer for comfort and aid. Then, she helped her grandmother to her feet.

"We have to fight for her, *Mammi*. We can't let her go," Susanna said.

"*Ja*, we've got to do everything in our power to keep this *boppli* safe. And we must have faith. Go now. Go help Seth. And remember to have faith and the Lord will provide a way," *Mammi* said.

As Susanna hurried downstairs, she was filled with misgivings. Snatching up her warm woolen cloak, she longed to believe what *Mammi* said. Surely *Gott* wouldn't abandon them now, when they needed Him most. But Susanna saw no way out of this predicament. They were going to lose Miriam forever. Unless they could prove Seth was the father. And he'd said that wasn't likely.

Susanna stepped out onto the front porch, knowing trust was difficult for her. It required courage, something she wasn't sure she had anymore. But trust was what she needed the most right now. She hadn't believed in any man for a very long time. But now, she believed in Seth. As she walked toward the waiting buggy, she forced herself to exercise faith. She owed that much to the Lord. And to Seth, who needed her now more than ever.

Seth couldn't believe this was happening. After everything he and Miriam had gone through, this was his worst nightmare come true. He was going to lose his sweet little daughter forever. And there wasn't a single thing he could do to stop it from happening.

Sitting in the buggy, he gripped the leather lead lines tighter as he urged the horse into a faster trot. They turned down the dirt lane leading to Bishop Yoder's farm. The carriage bounced and dipped as it struck the numerous mud puddles lining the road. No doubt, as the day gave way to night, the temperature would drop and the water would freeze to ice. Another storm was on its way and he was eager to get Susanna home before it struck. But first, he must meet with the bishop. He needed his advice. Badly.

"Maybe I could take Miriam and leave town. We could go somewhere far away where they can't find us," he said, speaking mostly to himself.

Susanna sat beside him on the front seat, her hands clasped tightly together in her lap. She stared straight ahead, her stubborn chin locked hard with purpose. For some reason, her presence brought him a great deal of comfort. He was glad she was here and he wasn't alone.

"You can't run away from this, Seth," she said. "What kind of life would that be for you and Miriam? Always on the run. How would you live? They'd find you and take Miriam away for sure. You might even end up in jail. And then, what would become of your *dochder*?"

She was right, of course. But what would become of his Miriam if she went to live with this stranger? Seth couldn't lose her. He just couldn't! And in his heart, he carried a prayer, asking *Gott* for help.

"Let's wait and see what the bishop suggests. He'll know what you should do," she said.

He nodded, keeping his eyes on the narrow road. Her advice was sound. Just having Susanna here with him now gave him the faith and confidence he needed to deal with this problem. Without a father of his own, Bishop Yoder was the next best thing. He would know what Seth should do.

"*Ja*, you're right," Seth said, hoping it was true.

But in his heart, he was more than worried. The bishop was just a man, after all. He had no control over the law of the land. And the last thing Seth wanted was to get crosswise with the *Englisch* authorities.

They pulled up in front of the bishop's log farmhouse. Like many of their people, Seth knew Bishop Yoder had built the home with his own two hands from a kit he had ordered locally. Ominous gray clouds filled the sky overhead. They must get back into town soon.

Seth hopped out of the buggy and went around to help Susanna down. Chickens scattered in a flurry, squawking their disapproval.

Bishop Yoder came from the barn carrying a metal bucket. Seeing them, he set the container on top of a water barrel and greeted them. He was dressed in his warm winter garb, and his breath appeared like puffs of smoke on the frigid air.

"*Guder daag!* What brings you out to my place on such a cold afternoon?" the bishop called in his deep, cheerful voice.

With a long, graying beard, the man had eyes that were usually filled with kindness. The bishop had been elected to his office by the members of their congregation because of his wisdom and compassion. As he came near, he must have seen the morose expressions on Seth's and Susanna's faces. He frowned, his bushy eyebrows drawing together over his gentle brown eyes.

"What is it? What has happened?" he asked.

"Bishop, I received this no more than an hour ago." Seth handed him the envelope and waited as he opened it and read the contents.

With a deep sigh, the bishop returned the papers to Seth, then reached up to squeeze his shoulder in an act of comfort. "*Komm* into the house. First, we will get you both something warm to drink. Then, we will sit down and talk."

Seth waited respectfully for Susanna to precede him up the narrow path leading to the bishop's front door. Though his mind was churning with doubts, Seth felt grateful to be among friends. But hope almost failed him. Neither Susanna nor the bishop could save Miriam for him.

Half an hour later, Bishop Yoder accompanied them back outside to Seth's waiting buggy. They'd had a good discussion, and the bishop had provided counsel and a reference.

"Try not to worry about this, Seth," the bishop said as he shook Seth's hand.

"I'll try. And I'll do as you advise and pay a visit to Carl Nelson first thing when I get back into town," Seth said.

Carl was one of two attorneys in Riverton. He was also Amish-friendly. Several of their people had sought his legal services over the years. The Amish trusted Carl, as much as they could trust any *Englisch* man.

Bishop Yoder nodded. "Don't worry about the cost. The *Gmay* will help you pay your fees, whatever they might be. The most important thing is to ensure Miriam stays with the Amish, where she can grow up feeling loved and cared for. We are her people and will do everything in our power to help you keep her."

Opening the passenger door to the buggy, Seth took Susanna's arm and helped her climb inside. Once she was settled, he closed the door and faced the bishop again. Susanna lowered her window, able to hear their parting words.

"*Danke*, bishop. I appreciate your help. More than I can say," Seth said.

The bishop smiled. "Keep me apprised. I'm happy to see you two getting along so well. You've been through a lot, losing your respective spouses. You both can use a *gut* friend right now. I'm glad you have each other to depend on."

Susanna's face flushed a pretty shade of pink that had nothing to do with the chilly breeze. Likewise, Seth wasn't sure what to make of the bishop's words. There seemed to be a veiled suggestion in his statement. But Seth had brought Susanna along for moral support and nothing else. They would never be a couple. They weren't even friends, just friendly business partners. That was all.

Or were people seeing them as more?

Seth walked around to the driver's side of the buggy. The bishop followed, reaching out to touch Seth's arm before he could open the door.

"Seth, just one more thing." The bishop leaned close and spoke low, so Susanna couldn't overhear his words. "I know you believe you are not Miriam's biological *vadder*. But remember the Lord can work miracles in our lives. Every day, I see amazing things come to pass that I never thought feasible. But with *Gott*, nothing is impossible. Don't forget prayer and to have faith. In the end, I have no doubt the Lord will make everything turn out for the best. But no matter what, you must have the strength of heart to accept His will in your life."

Gazing into this kind man's eyes, Seth nodded. He felt a softening inside his heart. For so long, he'd felt abandoned by *Gott*. Like he didn't matter and no one cared about him and Miriam. But now, as he joined Susanna inside the buggy, he felt stronger somehow. A warmth filled his chest and he felt comforted. He no longer felt alone.

As they rode into town, he vocalized a thought that occurred to him out of nowhere. "Maybe it would be best for Miriam to live with her real *daed*."

Even as he said the words, he knew it

wasn't true. No one could love Miriam more than he did. Not even her real father. Especially if Rob raised Miriam in a life of drugs and crime.

"*You* are Miriam's true *vadder*. That is what we must believe. That is what we must fight for. We can't accept anything less," Susanna said, her voice filled with firm conviction.

How he hoped it was true. But ultimately, he was the one who must fight. Susanna wasn't his wife. She wasn't Miriam's mommy. And she never would be. Maybe he was more alone than he thought.

"I tried to keep the possibility of Miriam's paternity a secret from everyone," he said. "Now that secret is out there, and the whole town will know. There's nothing I can do to stop gossip from spreading. But I can deal with that, as long as I know Miriam is safe."

"She will be. *Gott* will see to that," Susanna said with a nod of assurance.

He breathed out a big sigh. "I wish I had your and Bishop Yoder's faith. I don't know how you can be so strong."

She was quiet for a moment, staring straight ahead. Then, she spoke in a low voice that was roughened by emotion.

"You have let me know your secret, so I will

tell you mine," she said slowly, not looking at him. Her hands knotted in tight fists in her lap.

"Thomas used to get angry with me." She paused, and he wondered if she'd go on.

"Did he have a temper?" Seth asked.

"*Ja*, and he used it on me. He would…"

She couldn't seem to say it, so he added softly, "Beat you?"

Even as the words left his mouth, he hoped they weren't true.

"*Ja*, and more," she said, so softly he almost didn't hear her over the clop of the horse's hooves.

To his surprise, she told him all about Thomas. How he used to beat her and curse at her. How he drank himself into oblivion most nights and let their farm fall into disrepair. She couldn't go or do anything without his approval. Thomas had even attacked her in the chicken house, once. No wonder she'd been afraid of Seth that day when she'd been gathering eggs with little Miriam.

Seth was absolutely appalled. Now he understood the dilapidated condition of Susanna's farm and why she had never remarried. She wanted to retain her independence. Never again did she want any man to dominate, hurt or control her.

"I'm certain Thomas even caused his own death," she said. "He had consumed a lot of alcohol the day he died. I begged him not to go out into the fields in that condition but he wouldn't listen to me. I found him a couple of hours later. He was dead."

"What happened? How did he die?" he asked.

She shrugged as a solitary tear slid down her pale cheek. He almost reached over to wipe it away but stopped himself just in time.

"I'm not sure. I doubt I will ever know. All I can figure is he fell off the combine. The doctor said he struck his head very hard. He was just lying out in the field, his head bleeding. Luna and Billy, our two draft horses, were standing there, still harnessed to the machinery. I ran for help but it was too late."

"I'm so sorry, Susanna. I didn't know all of this. Especially the part about him abusing you," he said.

"No one did. I kept it a secret even from *Mammi*. It would break her heart if she knew Thomas had been beating me. And I ask that you not tell anyone, please. I don't want people to know the truth, especially when it no longer matters," she said.

He nodded. "Of course. I can understand

that. It's our secret. But how did you keep it hidden so well?"

She sighed. "When my arms were covered with bruises, I wore long sleeves to hide them. Thomas never hit me in the face because he knew our people would see the marks and know what he had done. I never told Bishop Yoder, either, but sometimes, I think he suspected the truth. So, you see? You are not the only one who has kept an ugly secret hidden away."

He gave a caustic laugh. "I guess not."

"After Thomas died, I felt so guilty because I… I was glad he was gone. And I know that's not how the Lord wants us to be." She glanced at Seth, looking embarrassed by her confession. "Please don't think badly of me for that."

He smiled. "Believe me, I don't. And can I tell you something else?"

She nodded.

"I felt the same way after Eve died. I was relieved because I knew her suffering and mine had finally ended," he said.

She looked at him, her eyes wide and her mouth hanging open in shock. "You did? You really felt that way, too?"

He nodded. "And like you, I felt guilty for it. I know it's not kind to be glad someone is gone. The Lord expects better from us. But I tried so hard to help Eve. I truly did."

She shook her head, a sad little smile curving her lips. "I did the same with Thomas. And I wish he had been half the man you are."

Now, it was Seth's turn to drop his mouth open in surprise. No one had ever paid him such a high compliment in all his life. But he couldn't tell Susanna that. It was too filled with *Hochmut*, too prideful. And right now, he was trying to be humble enough to accept *Gott*'s will in his life. But hearing her talk about the abuse she'd suffered caused a deepseated anger to build within Seth's chest. If Thomas were here right now, he would confront the man. And yet, Seth knew anger wasn't of *Gott*. He was trying hard to have a calm heart. But knowing he was in danger of losing his child filled him with dread.

"I wasn't always strong," Susanna said. "And for the longest time, I was furious and determined to remain aloof from the world. Now, I don't feel angry anymore. I just feel sorry for Thomas. He stole a lot of happiness from us," Susanna said.

Yes, that exactly described Seth's feelings toward Eve. With her poor choices, she had cheated them out of so much bliss. She didn't need to die young. It was such a waste.

"I realize now that we each need other people in our lives. *Gott* wants us to serve others. That's why I agreed to provide childcare for Miriam," Susanna said.

He nodded. "*Danke*, I'm glad you did. I'll always be grateful to you and Dorothy for that."

"If Eve and Thomas had made different choices, all our lives could have been so much different," she said.

Yes, it was true.

They rode the rest of the way in silence, each absorbed in their own thoughts. Seth dropped Susanna off at the store, so she could check on her grandmother and Miriam. Then, he hurried over to the attorney's office alone. He was beyond grateful to Susanna for her kind words and support. Her story touched his heart. She deserved a happy life and he wished he could do more for her. But he realized he couldn't take it any further. A relationship with another woman would only complicate his life even more. And right now, he must focus on saving Miriam. Nothing else mattered.

Chapter Ten

"All rise."

Susanna came to her feet. Standing just behind Seth and his attorney at the front of the small courtroom, she braced Miriam against her hip. It was snowing outside and she'd doffed their warm, winter shawls and scarves, setting them on the chair next to her with the diaper bag. The court bailiff had instructed her to sit here, in the spectator seats. The chairs were nothing more than hard metal with a tan cushion to pad the seat. In such a small court, there were no barricades or partitions. From what Susanna understood, this was a traveling judge out of the county seat in Cañon City, Colorado. He came to Riverton on a semimonthly basis to hear cases such as this one and to make rulings.

The bailiff was a middle-aged *Englisch*

woman with very short hair and wearing an official gray uniform. A variety of patches and badges were affixed to the sleeves and front of her starched shirt. On her hips, she wore a Taser, handcuffs, a radio and flashlight. Her shirt looked extra bulky. To her horror, Susanna realized the woman must be wearing a bulletproof vest. Susanna couldn't imagine doing a job that required such a thing and she wished she was back at the noodle shop with *Mammi*, who was minding the store for her.

The bailiff stood beside the raised dais. A door near the judge's bench opened and an older, distinguished-looking man with gray hair and spectacles and wearing long black robes entered the room.

"The honorable Clinton Cook presiding," the bailiff called to the room.

The judge came forward and sat in a tall-backed, cushioned chair at his bench. He reached for a pile of papers sitting in front of him, then nodded vaguely at the group before him. "Be seated, please."

They all sat. Susanna glanced over at the plaintiff's table, gazing surreptitiously at Rob Thompson, the man claiming to be Miriam's father. He was dressed in one of the formal suits, ties and shirts the *Englisch* were fond of wearing, but his hair was overly long and greasy. He had enough stubble on his cheeks and chin to indicate he hadn't shaved in a couple of days. His eyes were blue, like Miriam's, but he'd barely spared the child more than a backward glance as they'd entered the courtroom. As he sat forward, Rob's shoulders hunched, his expression one of sullen annoyance. Rob's attorney sat beside him, a man Susanna didn't recognize from town. Maybe he was from Cañon City. As directed, it was eight o'clock on Tuesday morning and the circuit court was now in session.

On the left side of the judge's bench were a witness stand and a cubicle for the court reporter, a young *Englisch* woman with long, painted fingernails who barely looked up as she tap-tapped away on her keyboard. Framing each side of the judge's seat were the American and state of Colorado flags.

For Susanna, it was an awkward, sterile room and she longed to hurry home as fast as possible. The only reason she was here was to tend Miriam while Seth faced the court. Sitting in front of her beside Carl Nelson, his lawyer, Seth glanced at her from over his shoulder. He didn't smile, his eyes filled with anxious concern. It was as if he was assuring himself that she and Miriam were here and doing okay.

"Let's see… This is Thompson versus Lehman. A paternity case." Judge Cook spoke to himself as he perused the papers in his hands. Finally, he set the pages aside and peered over the top of his spectacles at Seth, then Rob Thompson, as if assessing each man individually.

"I understand your deceased wife was the mother of the infant, is that right?" The judge looked directly at Seth, who nodded, holding his black felt hat in his lap.

"That's correct, Your Honor," Carl Nelson spoke in a loud, confident tone on behalf of Seth.

Judge Cook pivoted his head toward Rob Thompson. "And you are claiming to be the biological father?"

Rob nodded as his lawyer spoke for him. "That is correct, sir."

Susanna watched all of this with silent interest. But when the judge looked directly at her and Miriam, she gulped.

"And is this the child in question?" Judge Cook asked.

Susanna didn't answer, grateful when Carl spoke for her.

"Yes, sir. This is Miriam. She's eleven months old now," Carl said.

As if she knew they were discussing her, the little girl chose that moment to look right at the judge, wave her arms rapidly and babble something only she could understand. Judge Cook's features softened and the corners of his mouth almost lifted in a smile. Almost.

"All right, then. Let's see if we can determine who this little girl belongs to." Judge Cook cleared his throat and became all businesslike. "Within the next week, both of you gentlemen will report to a lab in Pueblo for a paternity test. Miriam will also be taken to the lab and be tested in that time frame. We'll then meet back here on…" The judge leaned to the side as the court reporter pointed at the computer screen. "We'll meet again on December twenty-second at ten o'clock in the morning. At that time, this court will notify you of who the biological father is. In the meantime, the infant will not be permitted to stay with either the plaintiff or the defendant. She will need to be temporarily placed in another home until we can get this sorted out. Is there a neutral party who is not related to the baby that she can stay with?" He looked at Susanna again.

"Yes, sir," Carl began. "This is Susanna

Glick. She is no blood relation to Miriam and has been providing childcare for the baby on a regular basis. Miriam already knows Susanna well and is comfortable with her. We ask the court to allow the baby to stay with her."

The judge rested an elbow against his desk and leaned forward as his gray eyes peered at Susanna. "Are you willing to keep the infant in your custody at all times, both day and night, until this matter can be resolved?"

Susanna took a deep, settling breath and nodded. "Yes, sir, I am."

The lawyer had warned them that the judge might want to place Miriam with a neutral party, someone who didn't have a stake in her custody, but Susanna hadn't believed he'd actually take the baby from Seth right away. This situation posed all kinds of inconvenience for her. When Susanna had agreed to look after Miriam, she hadn't signed on for nighttime care as well.

She didn't want to be here. Didn't want to get embroiled in Seth's troubles. But he was in a tight spot. There was no way Susanna was going to refuse to help and have Miriam sent to stay with strangers in some *Englisch* foster home. Not if she could stop it from happening.

Judge Cook's eyes narrowed and his bushy

eyebrows lowered in a stern frown. "Miss Glick, until this court determines paternity of this infant, the two men may visit the baby but they are to have supervised visits only. Miriam is not to be left alone with either man at any time whatsoever. Nor are you to leave this jurisdiction with the child for any reason. Do you understand this responsibility as I've explained it?"

She nodded. "Yes, sir. I do."

Looking over at Seth, she met his gaze. He appeared so stoic and worried, his eyes resting on her and the baby. His jaw was locked hard as granite and he looked almost desperate. She didn't know what he would do if Miriam was taken from him and given to Rob Thompson.

In contrast, Susanna noticed that Rob didn't even look at Miriam. Since he was claiming to be the child's father, that seemed rather odd. Wouldn't a real dad be curious about his own daughter? Shouldn't he want to gaze at her with amazement and learn every movement, every nuance and contour of her face? Instead, Rob seemed completely disinterested in the child. And there was an ugly spirit about him that Susanna couldn't quite put her finger on. As if this whole proceeding was a nuisance he had to tolerate. Miriam didn't seem to be his focus, but rather a means to an end.

Oh, dear. Susanna had a bad feeling about this. Frequently, Thomas had treated her this same way. As if he was disinterested and didn't care about her, but he had to put up with her anyway. And for that reason, Susanna didn't believe Rob cared about Miriam. Which led her to wonder why he wanted the little girl. What possible reason could he have for putting them all through this awful court hearing? It didn't make sense. Not to Susanna.

"Fine. We'll reconvene on the twenty-second when paternity will be settled." Judge Cook picked up a wooden gavel and smacked it hard against his desk in finality.

Susanna flinched at the sound, immediately coming out of her musings. She gathered up her and the baby's things while Seth leaned close and spoke with Carl for several moments. Then, Seth came to escort her out of the courtroom.

"Carl is going to check on a few things and asked us to wait outside for him." Seth lifted an arm to indicate the exit.

Bundling the baby up nice and warm, Susanna carried her into the outer room where other *Englisch* people from town sat waiting to be called into court for their own hearings. Seeing she was Amish, some of them stared at her with curiosity. From the wide picture windows, Susanna could see it had stopped snowing. Though it was cold, they were wrapped up warm and she longed to escape this horrible building. But Rob stood beside the door leading to the parking lot. She would have to walk past him to leave.

As if reading her thoughts, Seth cupped her elbow with his hand. "*Komm* on, I'll put you and Miriam inside my buggy. I've got a nice, heavy quilt there and can wrap you both up so you won't be cold. I think you'll be safe and warm enough to wait there until I'm sure Carl doesn't need me here anymore. It shouldn't be more than a few minutes before I can take you *heemet*."

"*Ja*, I'd prefer to wait out there," Susanna said, appreciating his thoughtful insight.

They stepped over to the door and Susanna was prepared to dart outside quickly, hoping to avoid any words with Rob. But it wasn't to be. Seth held the door open for her but Rob shot out an arm to hold her back. She immediately stepped aside, forcing Seth to let go of the door and step back inside. Seth inserted himself between her and Rob and she thought it was a protective gesture, to shield her and the baby from Rob. As the two men faced each other, she caught their tight, furious expressions. The Amish were pacifists and didn't believe in fighting. But right now, Seth's countenance was one of pure rage. His hands tightened into fists at his sides. She'd seen this kind of fury in Thomas's eyes before, just before he'd lashed out at her. And once more, she doubted Seth. Would he strike Rob? Or turn the other cheek and walk away. She truly didn't know what he might do.

"I found out about Eve's death when I saw her obituary in *The Budget*," Rob said.

Seth gazed at the man without blinking. All he could think was this was the man who had helped keep Eve addicted to illicit drugs. She'd told Seth all about it. For just a moment, a piercing rage swept through Seth's body. He was so angry that he was trembling with the impact. But then, he reminded himself of how the Savior wanted him to act and he forced himself to let the fury subside.

The Budget was a monthly newspaper dedicated to reporting stories about Amish and Mennonite people around the world. Not many *Englischers* subscribed to the periodical and Seth was surprised. Now, he knew how Rob found out about Eve's death. But why did he want Miriam so much? The guy had barely looked at the little girl. In fact, right now, with Susanna standing next to him, holding the baby in her arms, Rob didn't even glance at the child.

"Excuse me. We'd like to leave now," Seth said, indicating the door that Rob was blocking. Seth didn't feel that Rob's comment merited a response and he wasn't about to stand here and chat with the guy.

"You're gonna have to give me that baby. It's just a matter of time." Rob spoke low enough that no one else in the waiting room could hear, except for him and Susanna.

"We will wait for the judge's final decision on that," Seth said, forcing himself to speak in an even tone.

From all outer appearances, Seth remained quiet and nonconfrontational. But inside, he was more than upset. The Lord had taught him to have a peaceful heart. But how could he remain calm when he might lose his little girl?

Rob leaned forward and it was all Seth could do not to flinch or draw away. Instead, Seth remained passive but stood his ground. He didn't budge an inch. He was a man, after all, and he wasn't about to back down. But neither would he use physical force.

"I'll tell you what," Rob whispered. "You pay me ten thousand dollars and I'll make this paternity suit disappear. It's that simple. You give me money and I won't take the baby away from you."

To add emphasis to his words, Rob clicked his fingers, as if he were performing a magic trick that would make all this trouble evaporate. Seth wished it was that simple.

Overhearing Rob's words, Susanna gasped in outrage and shifted the baby in her arms. Rob looked her way.

"Ah, what a cute little baby," Rob said.

He reached out and tapped Miriam's chin overly hard with his index finger. The baby promptly burst into tears and pressed her face against Susanna's throat, as if she was frightened of the man.

Rob sneered at the child. "You little brat."

"No! She's not a brat. She's an innocent child," Susanna said.

Turning her back on the man, she shielded Miriam from his view and spoke in *Deitsch* as she comforted the little girl.

"There, there, *Liebchen*. I'm here. It's *allrecht*," she cooed.

Seth couldn't believe what the man had said. Rob had just offered to drop the paternity suit if Seth paid him ten thousand dollars. It was so tempting to accept Rob's offer. But Seth knew the man would just turn up again and again, demanding more and more money. That's how drug addicts worked. They were willing to lie, cheat and steal…anything to get their next fix. And eventually, Seth wouldn't be able to pay the money. And what then? They'd be right back here in court, facing more paternity tests and the court's final judgment. It was better to get it over with now. But discovering that all Rob cared about was money upset Seth more than he could say. Finally, he understood what this was all about. And in his heart, Seth begged *Gott* not to let this travesty of justice occur. He didn't know how to work it out, but he couldn't just hand Miriam over to such a vile man.

"Think about it and I'll be in touch," Rob said, a wide smirk crossing his face.

The man stepped away from the door, walking over to join his own attorney as he and Carl came out of the courtroom.

Carl joined Seth and Susanna and they stepped outside with the baby. A portico sheltered them and protected their feet from the damp slush covering the walk paths.

"Okay, the next hearing is all set," Carl said, looking at Seth. He handed him a paper with an address on it. "In the next week, you'll go to this lab for your tests and we'll meet back here in December for the final decision. In the meantime, Miriam shouldn't be alone with you." He looked at Susanna. "Mr. Thompson might try to contact you for visitation of Miriam. Don't let the baby be alone with him, either."

"Don't worry. I won't," Susanna said.

Seth quickly told the man about Rob's offer if Seth paid him ten thousand dollars. "He doesn't want Miriam. He just wants money."

Carl nodded, his face filled with sadness. "I was afraid of that. The man has quite a record of drug abuse and petty larceny. He's not a good character. Certainly not father material."

"How can the judge even consider turning Miriam over to such an evil man?" Susanna asked quietly.

Carl shrugged and zipped his warm winter coat up to his throat. "Criminals have children, too. This is a paternity case. Nothing else matters, except proving who is Miriam's biological father. His prior police record has no bearing in this matter, and the judge would not be pleased if I brought it up." He grimaced. "I know it's not fair."

"But if you tell the judge about Rob's blackmail, won't he listen to reason?" Seth asked.

"Nope," Carl said. "I'm very sorry, but that's hearsay. It's not pertinent to this hearing and would be considered unethical for me to even tell the court about Rob's actions. All the judge cares about in this case right now is the paternity result. It's science and nothing more. If Rob is Miriam's biological father, the judge will have no choice but to hand her over to him. Then, if Rob abuses or neglects Miriam or exposes her to illicit drugs or other crimes at a later time, that is another case entirely. He could very well end up being deemed an unfit father in the future, but first the judge has to decide who is the actual father and award custody of Miriam accordingly."

Feeling outraged by the lack of justice in this situation, Seth shook his head. "You're not serious."

"I am very serious, Seth," Carl said. "It's the law. At this point, my hands are tied. Just get the paternity tests and let's see what the results reveal. Then, we can go from there. If you have any questions between now and our next court date, you know where to find me. Have a happy Thanksgiving!"

Turning, Carl stepped gingerly over the

drifts of snow and hurried to his car in the parking lot. Seth and Susanna stood there, watching him go. Realizing he was completely at the mercy of the court didn't sit well with Seth. He felt so helpless and let down. All he had left was his faith in *Gott*.

"*Komm* on. Let's go. This cold air isn't *gut* for you or the *boppli*," he said.

Without response, Susanna headed toward his waiting buggy.

He helped her and the baby climb inside, then went around to the driver's seat and took the leather leads into his hands. They all sat there for several minutes. Seth felt immobile and shocked. This couldn't be happening. Not to Miriam, an innocent and sweet child. And yet, Seth knew *Gott* gave all men and women their free agency to choose their actions. And frequently, those choices hurt other people, too.

"I'm terrified my innocent child might end up in Rob's hands. But what can I do to stop it?" he finally spoke the words out loud.

"Have faith. Trust in *Gott*'s will. If we do what's right, it will all turn out in the end. I just know it will," came Susanna's soft reply.

He glanced at her, surprised to see tears sparkling in her eyes. "You sound so certain and sure. I wish I had your faith," he said.

She showed a weak smile and brushed at her eyes. "You do. You're just being tried right now, so it isn't easy for you. It's not easy for any of us. But we will come through this okay. I can't believe we won't."

He nodded, realizing she was also upset at the prospect of losing Miriam. It just didn't seem right.

"Finally, I understand Rob's motivation to put us all through this charade of a court hearing. It's not because he loves Miriam and values his own child. He just wants money," Susanna said.

"*Ja*, I don't think he's a *gut* man with *gut* motives," Seth agreed. "If I had ten thousand dollars, I'd give it to him, just to put an end to all of this misery."

She tilted her head and looked at him with doubt. "I have no doubt Bishop Yoder and our congregation would get you the money. But if you paid it, Rob would only demand more later on."

Seth stared out the windshield, at the swirling snow starting to fall again. He needed to get them home. "You're right. But I'm out of options. Maybe I should pay the money, then take Miriam and run away. I could return to my *familye* in Indiana. It'd be difficult

for Rob to find us there. If I can just protect
Miriam until she's a grown woman, then it
won't matter anymore."

"That is an option but Rob might pursue
you there, too. If he gets the law involved,
they could track you down and arrest you,"
she said.

"You're right, of course. You're always
right, Susanna." He looked at her and forced
a smile. And in that moment, he realized he
valued her opinion more than that of anyone
he'd ever met.

She looked away, as if she felt uncomfortable being here with him. He knew this was a
huge imposition on her. She was so busy and
now she would need to keep Miriam with her
day and night, until the results of the paternity tests could be determined.

"For now, I will stand and face whatever
comes of this. Do you need me to load up Miriam's crib and take it to your farm?" he asked.

She shook her head. "*Ne*, I already have
one there. It belonged to Thomas's *mudder*.
It's old but is clean and should suffice for the
next few weeks."

It seemed everything was settled. Now,
they just needed to go to the testing center
in Pueblo for the paternity tests. Seth had

no idea what all that entailed. He hated the thought of a doctor poking Miriam to take her blood, or whatever they needed to do to get their biological results. But it couldn't be helped. A court of law had mandated it.

Releasing the brake, he slapped the leads against the horse's rump and the buggy lurched forward. They rode in relative silence.

When they arrived at the store, Miriam was sound asleep in Susanna's arms. Without a word, Seth helped her out of the buggy.

"Danke," she said before carrying his daughter inside.

Watching her go, Seth was filled with misgivings. There were so many words he longed to say to Susanna. So many tangled feelings spiraling around inside him. But he couldn't seem to sort them out.

Maybe later, once this horrible paternity case was resolved, he could speak with Susanna in private. Maybe then, he'd know how he felt about her and how to proceed. But right now, all he could think about was Miriam and saving her from being dragged away to a home filled with strangers who didn't love her. He couldn't think about Susanna and her sweet, gentle ways. Not until he knew Miriam was safe.

Chapter Eleven

Thanksgiving was a subdued affair. Susanna and Mammi made a beautiful roast turkey with all the trimmings and shared their meal with Seth and Miriam. No one spoke much. The air seemed charged with a morose undercurrent of doubt and misgivings. As Susanna sat at the table in her kitchen and spooned mashed potatoes into the baby's mouth, she remembered all the things she was grateful for. Her blessings were many, yet she couldn't help thinking that she'd give it all up, if only Miriam could remain safely at home with Seth.

The following morning, Bob Crawley, a jovial *Englisch* man who frequently drove the Amish long distances in his car, picked them up at the noodle store promptly at eight o'clock. Susanna had been up early, decorating the shop. Green pine boughs, tied red ribbons and battery-operated candles filled each windowsill. A wreath of greenery and pine cones hung on the front door. The zesty fragrance of cinnamon and allspice filled the air, giving the shop a warm feeling of *familye* and Christmas. And yet, Susanna felt down in the dumps. Their errand today was anything but pleasant.

Standing at the front door, Susanna was wrapped in her warm winter shawl as she held the baby in her arms. Seth was outside, speaking to Bob. She glanced at the blue vehicle with misgivings. While she'd traveled in a large bus before, this would be her first time riding in a car. *Mammi* would remain behind to mind the store.

"Are you sure you can handle everything on your own? Since it's Black Friday, the shop will be busy today," she told her grandmother.

"It's always busy. I'll be fine. Our shelves are filled to capacity, so we have lots of merchandise to sell. And Seth needs you more than me," *Mammi* said.

"*Ja*, the judge ordered me not to let the *boppli* be alone with him until this paternity case has been resolved. I have to go. You'll be on your feet a lot today. Be sure to sit down and rest when you can."

She was worried about *Mammi*. With it being one of the heaviest business days of the year, Susanna feared they might be flooded with Christmas shoppers.

"I will. Stop worrying." *Mammi* handed Susanna the diaper bag they'd prepared earlier that morning.

The elderly woman opened the door and smiled. A blast of wintery air struck them but *Mammi* didn't seem to notice, in spite of not wearing a coat.

Susanna walked out onto the front step. "I shouldn't be gone long. Pueblo is only sixty miles away. But I have no idea how long the tests might take."

"I'll be fine. You go on now. And try to have some fun." *Mammi* leaned in for a quick hug, then went back inside and closed the door.

Susanna turned and saw Seth walking toward her. Wearing his black felt hat and a warm winter coat, he looked handsome in the brisk morning air. Always attentive, he reached out and took the diaper bag from her.

"Is everything *allrecht*?" he asked quietly as he cupped her elbow and accompanied her along the icy path to the car.

They'd received a heavy snowfall two days earlier, but he'd shoveled and spread ice melt along the walkways. It was still early in the morning and slick out. Since she didn't want to fall while carrying the baby, she didn't shrug him off.

"*Ja*, everything is as *gut* as a root canal from the dentist," she quipped.

He laughed. "You make a *gut* point. I'd rather we were going to Pueblo for some fun. But with the task ahead of us, I'm glad you're here with Miriam and me."

His words startled her and she glanced at his face. He was smiling but it didn't quite meet his eyes. She knew him well enough to realize he was doing his best to remain upbeat. But deep inside, he must be trembling with fear over the thought of losing his child. And for that reason alone, she was determined to remain positive, if only to help make this difficult time a bit easier for him.

She took a deep, settling breath and let it go. "Don't worry. *Gott* is in control and it's all going to work out fine."

He nodded, his mouth curved in that lopsided smile of his. "I know, but it's still rather difficult."

Yes, it was. If only she could believe her own words. But speaking such things out loud gave her added courage to believe in her faith.

She slid into the back and strapped Miriam into her safety seat, which Seth had put there minutes earlier. While Seth showed her how to strap on her own seat belt, she avoided meeting his eyes. He leaned over her and his warm hands brushed against hers as she fought with the buckle and learned how the contraption worked. Then, he flashed a smile of encouragement before closing her door. He sat in the front with Bob, a jolly man in his early forties with an overly loud voice and a penchant for conversation. As the car pulled away from the curb, Susanna gripped the armrest and held her breath. The car seemed to zip along at lightning speed as it headed outside town and onto the freeway. Wintry fields of white flashed past her window and she wondered how the *Englisch* could stand to go so fast all the time.

Seth tossed a quick glance at her from over his wide shoulder.

"You *allrecht* back there?" he asked again.

She nodded, biting her tongue to keep from begging him to let her out right now. He must be frantic with worry, yet here he was looking after her welfare. Always kind, always considerate. So very different from how Thomas had been.

For almost an hour, Susanna didn't say a word. Listening to the persistent roar of the car engine and the two men's voices as they chatted in the front seat, she kept Miriam entertained with a rag doll *Mammi* had made for her and a teething ring. And when they arrived in Pueblo, Bob drove them directly to the DNA testing center and pulled up to the sidewalk.

"Here you are. You take the ladies inside," Bob said. "I'll go park the car, then wait for you in the reception area while you take care of your business."

"Thank you." Seth climbed out and immediately opened Susanna's door.

After removing the baby from her car seat, Susanna looped the diaper bag over her arm and stepped out onto the curb. As Bob pulled away, she faced Seth. Her misgivings must have shown on her face, for he took hold of her arm again. It hadn't snowed as much here in Pueblo, but the paths were still damp. Together, they walked toward the tall, red brick building. Several *Englisch* people were coming and going from the parking lot and stared at them and their unique clothing. Susanna was used to such rude looks and ignored them.

Inside the waiting room, Seth helped her and the baby find a seat, then he stepped up to the front counter to check in. Bob joined them minutes later, sitting nearby as he scanned his cell phone and waited. Within fifteen minutes, they were shuttled into a treatment room. A nurse came in carrying a tray with an assortment of vials and cotton swabs on it.

"Hello! My name is Nurse Julie. I'll need to see some sort of ID. And will you fill this out for me, please?" She handed a pen, clipboard and paperwork to Seth.

"I'm afraid I don't have a driver's license, but I have our birth certificates and my library card. Will that suffice?" he asked.

Julie nodded. "The court sent over the request and said we could accept that kind of documentation in your case."

Ah! Susanna figured they didn't have many Amish paternity cases and she was grateful the judge had taken their special circumstances into account since Seth didn't drive a car.

While he filled in the pages, the nurse smiled at Miriam. "And who is this little cutie-pie?"

Seeming shy, Miriam ducked her head against Susanna's chest and gazed in a side-long glance at the nurse.

"This is Miriam," Susanna said.

"Miriam. What a beautiful name. Can you set her up here, please?" Julie glanced at Susanna and patted a bench where a thin piece of crinkly paper had been spread for the new patient.

Susanna did as asked and removed the hood from the baby's warm bunting to reveal her tiny white prayer *kapp*. Then, she stepped to the side so Julie could access the baby.

"Ah, you're such a little beauty," Julie said as she removed a cotton swab from a sanitary pouch.

The nurse smiled and cajoled Miriam, quickly swabbing each of the baby's inner cheeks. Startled by the dry stick in her mouth, Miriam drew away, her little chin trembling. She looked like she was about to cry as she reached for Susanna.

"Mammi!" she cried.

Susanna's heart melted. Julie hadn't hurt Miriam at all but, knowing the gravity of the situation, it was all Susanna could do not to snatch up the child and race out of the room.

Tears streamed down Susanna's face and she brushed them aside as he picked up the baby and comforted her.

She offered another silent prayer for help

and realized, against her will, she had fallen in love with both Miriam and Seth. She wasn't just his friend or Miriam's caretaker. She was in love with him and couldn't imagine being separated from either of them.

How had this happened? She'd promised herself she would never love another man. Yet, here it was. An emotion she couldn't stop to save her life. She loved Seth. She did. More than she'd ever loved anyone else in her life. She couldn't deny it. She could hardly stand to lose him or Miriam.

"You're all done, sweetie. You see? That wasn't so bad, now. Was it?" Julie spoke in a pleasant voice as she caressed Miriam's little arm in a soothing gesture.

Still smiling, Julie slid the swab stick into a clear vial and sealed it with a rubber lid and sticky label. Stepping across the room, she slid the vial inside a sealed box. Susanna realized the added security meant that no one could tamper with the sample. Not without prying open the box. There was no way she or Seth could take the vial away, not that they would try to do such a thing. No doubt the judge would just order another test. Susanna had no doubt some people would resort to such subversion. But not her and Seth. Dishonesty defied the tenets of their faith. They just wanted this over with and Miriam safely at home where she belonged.

Julie faced Seth. "Okay, it's your turn, Mr. Lehman. Can you stand right here and I'll swab your cheeks, too?"

The woman pointed at a spot next to the bench where she'd set the tray of vials and cotton swabs.

Looking rather stoic, Seth moved into position and opened his mouth. Within moments, he was finished with his test.

"You're right. That wasn't bad," he said, glancing at Miriam with a look of relief.

"They've got these tests highly refined now. We used to have to take blood samples. These swab tests are very accurate and much less painful for the kiddies," Julie said.

She moved away as she labeled and closed up Seth's vial. As she had done with Miriam's test sample, she placed it in the sealed box.

Julie turned to face them. "That's it. I've got what I need and you're free to go."

"When will you know the results?" Seth asked.

Julie lifted one shoulder and showed a half smile of compassion. Surely she had no knowledge about their situation. She was merely a nurse facilitating the tests. But she seemed to understand the angst they were all feeling.

"The lab will probably have the results in three to five days. But I'm afraid you won't hear the results until your next court date. That's usually how it's done," she said.

Seth nodded and breathed out a quick exhale. "I see. Thank you."

Turning toward Susanna, he reached for the diaper bag and opened the door as she carried the baby out into the hallway. As she headed toward the front lobby, she walked fast, feeling a sense of freedom. They had the testing behind them but must wait for Seth's court date just before Christmas to find out the results. Right now, though, her new realization was troubling her even more.

She loved Seth. She loved his little daughter. But even if the paternity results came back in Seth's favor, it didn't help Susanna one iota. Her mind would be at ease knowing Miriam was with a father who loved her. But where did that leave Susanna and Seth?

Nowhere!

She had loved Thomas once, too. And look how that turned out. Even if Seth was interested in her, loving him didn't mean she wanted to marry him. She realized many Amish couples worked as a team, honoring and respecting one another. But not all marriages turned out that way. Susanna knew that firsthand. For the Amish, loving a man usually meant marriage and loss of freedom for a woman. And right now, love was not a strong enough inducement for her to cast aside her independence and tie herself to another man. She must be content with her life as it was. Never could she tell Seth how she felt about him. Not in a million years. Because once she did, there would be no turning back.

Stepping outside into the parking lot, Seth took a deep, cleansing breath and let it go. Looking up at the gray, sullen sky, he was more than ready to go home.

As they all loaded into Bob's car, Seth noticed a man standing on a tall ladder as he hung a string of lights along the pillars outside. Another man hung green bows laden with large red and gold Christmas balls and ribbon along the edge of the portico leading to the front doors of the testing center. He was whistling a happy Christmas carol as he worked. Everything looked so cheerful, a stark contrast to Seth's mood. Seth reminded himself that this was the season of the Christ child's birth and he tried to have faith. But deep inside, he felt nothing but a hollow ache in his heart.

The ride home to Riverton was solemn and quiet. Even Bob seemed to know the occupants of his car weren't interested in his incessant chatter.

"Did everything go okay with the testing?" Bob asked in a kind voice as they headed out of town.

Conscious of Susanna and Miriam riding quietly in the back seat, Seth nodded. "Yes, as well as could be expected."

Bob inclined his head. "Well, don't worry, then. You've done the best you can do. It's in God's hands now. He'll take care of you."

Seth jerked and looked at the man, feeling surprised. He hadn't told Bob about their situation, but driving to a DNA clinic, the man must know there was a problem. Seth had been raised to think the *Englischers* were hedonists who didn't really believe in God. Now, he realized that wasn't accurate. He hoped what Bob said was true and *Gott* was looking out for them. But when he had received his cheek swab, he hadn't held out much hope. He wasn't Miriam's biological father. He couldn't be. Could he? Fearing he was about to lose his precious daughter, his heart was breaking in two.

He glanced over his shoulder at Miriam and turned his body so he could watch her for a few moments. She was strapped securely into her seat and wore a warm padded black snowsuit. To protect her from the cold air, Susanna had pulled the hood up over the baby's head and folded a soft blanket around the child for good measure. Susanna always took such great care of Miriam.

All Seth could see was the child's little face as she snuggled against Susanna's side. The woman was leaning into the tiny girl and had one arm draped over the top of the safety seat, as if she didn't want to take her hands off the little tot. When Miriam saw him looking her way, she smiled wide and shot out a little hand toward him.

"Dat!" she cried.

Seth's heart went all soft and mushy inside. Surely this was his child, wasn't she? It took more than one of the *Englischer*'s biological tests to determine the best parent for Miriam, but he feared the imminent outcome would not be in his favor. And in the end, he knew the court would take away his little

girl. Despite Rob Thompson's criminal record, he could still be Miriam's father, and
the judge couldn't arbitrarily give a man's
daughter away. Rob was innocent of being
an unfit father until proved otherwise after
he had custody, and it knifed Seth's heart as
he thought of what that meant for Miriam.
And there was nothing he could do to stop it
from happening.

When Miriam had received her cheek
swab, he'd watched Susanna comfort her. Susanna was more of a mother to his daughter
than Eve had ever been. She took excellent
care of the baby. And he realized, since Susanna had come into his life, an orderly structure had taken hold of his world. Everything
was tidy and in its place, his laundry washed,
his apartment cleaned, with regular, nourish-
ing meals on the table. Susanna would make
some man an excellent wife one day. So, why
did the thought of Susanna marrying someone else bother him so much?

He met Susanna's gaze and saw the sad uncertainty in her eyes. She seemed to mirror
his own emotions.

He'd been so firm in his conviction that he
would never marry again. Now, he wasn't so
sure. But once the court took Miriam from

him, he'd have no need of a wife. And losing both Eve and Miriam, he'd be of no use to anyone.

He'd be well and truly alone.

That thought caused him to turn around and face forward.

And just like that, he realized he'd fallen in love with Susanna. She'd become more than a nanny for his daughter. More than just a friendly business partner. She'd become a close friend and confidante. Someone he trusted more than anyone else besides the Lord. She'd comforted him and he'd pushed her away. Too hurt to let another woman into his heart.

In that moment, he felt so lonely. Like he was losing everything he ever cared about. First, he'd lost his wife. Now, he was losing his daughter. And once they took Miriam away, he'd lose any possible future with Susanna, too. Except for her to pay rent on the store, he wouldn't even see her very often. He felt so broken inside that he didn't think he could ever offer her the love and devotion she was entitled to. Even if he was inclined to offer marriage, he was too battered and scarred inside to be any kind of good husband to her. She deserved so much more than he could offer.

Chapter Twelve

Seth scooped another forkful of hay and tossed it into the horse stall. Mack and Zelda, his two Percheron draft horses, ducked their heads over the trough and starting munching away.

Leaning against the handle of his pitchfork, he watched them for several moments. It was late afternoon and time for evening chores. Usually, there was something calm and soothing about working in his barn. Normally, he loved it here. But today, it did nothing to soothe his riotous feelings.

It had been two weeks since he and Miriam had received their tests at the DNA clinic in Pueblo. He wondered if the lab had the results yet. It didn't matter. They'd never divulge the findings to him. Not until their court date in a couple more weeks. Though he'd tried to stop thinking about it, he couldn't seem to get his mind off the issue. Was he Miriam's father? Or would they take her away from him?

He hefted another forkful of hay to the horses, trying to take his mind off his fears. He'd been spending longer and longer hours out in the fields. The extra work showed. Both his and Susanna's farms looked great. The houses had been painted, fences standing tall, and everything tidy and in its place. He even had their machinery ready and waiting for spring plowing and planting. But that was several months away. He needed something else to occupy his mind now.

Glancing to the side, he noticed through the crack in the doorway that dusk was settling over the valley. They'd received two inches of snow several days earlier and an inch of rain yesterday. The slushy earth had frozen and melted and was nice and damp. He'd filled each of his and Susanna's water barrels. The moisture was a tremendous blessing. It would deteriorate the compost he'd spread so it would nourish the soil. Their summer crops should be better than ever. If only his private life could be as prosperous, he'd be a happy man. With Miriam staying over at Susanna's house all the time, he had no need to hurry home to his deserted apartment. There was nothing for him there. The place was way too quiet. Too lonely.

He'd continued taking his meals with the women and had come to cherish that time because he could hold and play with the baby. He hated that he couldn't be alone with his own child and felt like he was some heinous monster who couldn't be trusted with his daughter.

Susanna and Dorothy were always so kind but there was a subdued darkness overshadowing them now. He knew the women felt it, too. He could see it in their eyes. They were all worried about Miriam and uncertain about the future. Even the baby seemed fussier than usual, though Susanna claimed she was just teething. Earlier that evening, Seth had sat quietly at the table as Susanna handed the baby a raw carrot to chew on. Watching his daughter chomp down on the vegetable, he couldn't help wondering who would look after her sore gums once the court took her away from him. He couldn't imagine Rob treating Miriam with such kindness. Instead, Seth fretted over the baby's care. Who would give her a bath and prepare her bottles? Who would show her compassion and love? Who would teach her about *Gott* and her place in the world? The thought that she might be mistreated or abused in any way made him crazy with worry.

Ah! He had to get his mind off this topic. He'd check the water trough, to make sure the livestock had plenty to drink. Then, he'd go home and rest. Sleep was what he needed right now. Sleep and some answers.

Turning, he froze. A man stood in the doorway. Both of the barn doors had been pushed open wide, letting drafts of cold, winter air flood through the room. With the fading sunlight at the man's back, his face was shrouded in shadow and Seth couldn't make out his features. He wore a black knit cap pulled low across his forehead.

"Who are you?" Seth asked, taking a step closer.

"You don't recognize me?" The man chuckled and Seth saw the flash of his smile.

Rob Thompson!

Seth gripped the handle of the pitchfork tightly. His heart thudded in his chest and every vein in his body pulsed with angry energy. Why had Rob come here? As far as Seth was concerned, they had nothing to say to each other. Rob had caused a lot of trouble in Seth's life and the man didn't even want Miriam.

Rob pushed the barn doors closed, then stepped out of the shadows. His nose was red from the cold and he wore a tattered coat and muddy boots. Seth wondered if he'd walked here to his farm. Seth hadn't heard a car pull up outside, but he'd been rather lost in his own thoughts and may have missed the sound.

Rob's face was unshaven, with splotches of dirt on one cheek, as if he'd been lying on the ground. He eyed Seth's pitchfork and an expression of fear crossed his face. But there was no need. Seth was a pacifist and would never use force against anyone. Instead, Seth stabbed the pitchfork into a bundle of hay, then turned to face the man.

"Miriam's not here. What do you want?" Seth asked, forcing himself to remain calm.

"Really? You don't know?" Rob said, his lips curling in a heartless smile.

"You can't have Miriam. Not until the court proves paternity," Seth said.

Rob waved a hand in the air, as if he were tossing away rubbish. "I don't want your little brat. She means nothing to me."

Seth's heart felt as if it sank to the ground. A sick feeling overwhelmed his stomach. Looking at Rob, Seth felt a moment of pity for the man. His coat and blue jeans had holes in them and looked ragged and filthy. Like he'd been sleeping in the dirt. Eve had come home looking like this a time or two and Seth knew Rob must have been living rough on the street since he'd seen him last. If Rob proved to be Miriam's father, Seth could just imagine what would happen to the little girl. She'd be abandoned for who knew how long. Nothing to eat. No one to help her, until someone found her. Hopefully that would be in time to get her the care she needed. And Seth couldn't stand the thought of Miriam going through that.

"Do you need food? I can give you something to eat but nothing else," Seth said.

"I don't want food," Rob yelled.

Seth flinched at the anger in the man's voice. "Then, you'd better leave now."

"I'm not going anywhere, until I'm good and ready," Rob said.

Seth went very still, grateful that Miriam was safely over at Susanna's place. But he had a choice to make. He could force Rob to leave or endure this unwanted visit. Hopefully, it didn't turn ugly. In Rob's eyes, Seth saw desperation. And when the man lifted a trembling hand to rub against his bearded face, Seth realized Rob needed a fix. Right now. Seth had seen these symptoms many times before, when Eve came home, desperate for some drugs to ease the pains of withdrawal. But the last thing Seth wanted now was to get involved in Rob's drug habit.

"I've got nothing for you here. No drugs. Nothing. You should go." Seth reached for the grain bucket, trying to show a heavy modicum of disinterest. Hopefully Rob would take the hint and leave. No matter what, Seth was not going to be pulled into Rob's world.

Rob stepped closer. "Have you got some money? I know you Amish. You're all wealthy, stashing wads of cash underneath your mattresses. Give me some and I'll go away."

Seth blinked and looked at the man. How dare Rob come to his home and ask such a thing?

"As a matter of fact, I don't keep my money here. It's in the bank, which would be closed at this time of night. No matter what, I have no money for you. I'm not a wealthy man. Not at all," Seth said.

"Liar!"

Before Seth could react, Rob lashed out and struck Seth in the face. Seth was knocked backward into the straw, his black felt hat flying off his head. He grunted and sat up, his nose and left cheek aching. He tasted blood as he rubbed the wound, trying to gather his thoughts. He didn't have the chance to speak before Rob clasped handfuls of his shirt front and hauled him to his feet. Seth hung there, trying to get his footing. When he did, his hands tightened into fists.

Oh, how badly he wanted to fight back. He really did. But he knew that reaction was of the natural man. Jesus Christ had taught that all men should be peacemakers, no matter what. Seth knew he must love his enemies and anyone who would spitefully use him, which included Rob Thompson. And if Seth would belong to Christ, then he must not take upon himself the natural man and become an enemy to *Gott*. No matter what, he must not use force.

Relaxing his hands, Seth stared at Rob with absolute composure. He believed in *Gott* the Eternal Father. He believed in Jesus Christ and His teachings. But now was a moment of truth. Seth had to put his money where his mouth was and prove what he'd always said he believed.

"I have no money and no drugs here, Rob. I have only food and warmth that I can offer you. Why don't you *komm* to my home and I'll offer you some supper," Seth said, forcing himself to speak in a calm, even tone.

Rob's expression changed to one of incredulity. "Supper? Are you crazy? I don't want food."

"That's all I have. Or I can drive you to the hospital in town. They can offer you some medical care. It'd only take a moment to hitch up my buggy. Why don't you let me help you?"

"Help me? Why, you..."

Rob drew back his fist and Seth prepared himself to see stars. He hated the thought of taking a beating. He had work in the morning and didn't want to be laid up or worse. But if that's what he must endure, then so be it.

A sound and a blast of wintery wind came from the doorway. Rob turned.

"What is going on here?"

Bishop Yoder stood in the open doorway with Susanna. They were both dressed in their winter clothes. Beyond them, Seth could see the bishop's horse and buggy standing in the yard. In a rush, all Seth could think was how grateful he was that Miriam wasn't with them. But what were they doing here at this hour of the evening?

Rob let go of Seth, who fell back into the straw. As Rob turned to face them, Seth regained his balance and stood up, brushing straw off his clothes. Without another word, Rob hurried around the bishop and scuttled out the door and off into the night. Joining the bishop, Seth heard an engine starting up along the street in front of the noodle shop. As he peered out into the dark, he saw Rob driving away in a battered car that looked like it had seen many better days.

"Seth! You're bleeding." Reaching inside her plain brown purse, Susanna pulled out a clean tissue and hurried over to him, where she dabbed it against his lip.

"What's going on here?" Bishop Yoder asked again, looking rather stern.

Seth took the tissue from Susanna's hand and smiled. "Am I ever glad to see you two."

What an understatement! He thought Rob was going to beat him into a pulp. Never had Seth been so happy to see someone in his life. And once more, he realized how much of a blessing Susanna had been to him. She'd saved him many times over. But this time, she and the bishop had kept him from getting the stuffing knocked out of him. Literally. Because even if it meant he would lose Miriam, he was not going to fight back. A man's honor was who he was inside and how he acted when no one else was watching. And when Rob had attacked him, Seth had been determined not to lose his dignity, no matter what. If he wanted the Lord's help to keep Miriam with him, then he must exercise faith. Even if it meant he might lose his little girl. But boy! Was he ever happy to see Susanna right now.

"Wasn't that Rob Thompson?" Susanna asked, her body trembling with shock and outrage as she gestured toward the door.

"*Ja*, it was Rob, *allrecht*," Seth said.

He pressed the tissue against his face and, when he pulled it away, there was blood all over it. A smear of blood marred the front of his shirt, too. He tugged at a front tooth, as if testing to see if it was loose.

"Did he strike you?" the bishop asked, peering closely at Seth's face.

Seth nodded. "He wanted drugs or money to buy drugs, and I wouldn't give him any."

The bishop pursed his lips tightly together. "But you didn't fight back, either, did you?"

"*Ne*, I did not fight, though I must confess I wanted to. At first." Seth showed a wan smile and looked down, as if he were ashamed by the admission.

Bishop Yoder clapped a hand on Seth's back. "Good man!"

Susanna couldn't comprehend this turn of events. "I can't believe that horrible man came here for money and drugs. Who does he think he is?"

"He's a child of *Gott* who has lost his way. I wish I could do something for him, but he's just like Eve. He won't let anyone help him right now," Seth said.

Susanna couldn't believe Seth's words. Her body pulsed with outrage, yet he had compassion for Rob. She peered at Seth's face, to see if he was truly okay. He staggered and the bishop took hold of his arm.

"Are you unsteady on your feet? You don't have a concussion, do you?" the bishop asked.

Seth shook his head. "*Ne*, I'm fine. Really. He didn't hit me hard enough to knock me out, so I doubt I have a concussion. I've never been punched in the face like that or seen anyone that angry before. I think I'm just shaken by what happened."

Bishop Yoder chuckled. "*Ach*, that's understandable. Have you finished your evening chores, or is there something I can do?"

Seth shook his head. "*Ne*, I had just finished and was preparing to go *heemet* when Rob arrived."

"Then, let's get you there," Bishop Yoder said.

Though Seth seemed steady on his feet, Susanna took hold of his other arm and held on tight. Together, she and the bishop escorted Seth into the back kitchen of the noodle shop. She couldn't believe Rob had come here, looking for money to buy drugs. It indicated to her the lengths a drug addict would go to in order to get their next fix. And knowing how desperate Rob must be made her pity him. Like Eve, he needed specialized help to overcome his addiction. But holding Miriam hostage was not the answer to Rob's problems.

As they reached the stairs, Seth pulled away from them. "You don't need to mollycoddle me. I'm *allrecht*. He only hit me once." He took hold of the handrail as he walked upstairs. "If you hadn't arrived, I fear he would have beat me some more. I'm glad you came when you did. *Gott* always provides a way, doesn't He?"

As Susanna followed him upstairs, his words touched her heart. Here he was, so worried about losing his daughter, yet he exercised faith. Maybe Susanna should do the same. She saw no way out of this dilemma, yet the Lord could see the full picture. This life was not everything. There was so much more in store for them, if they only lived faithfully.

"Do you think Rob will *komm* back?" Susanna asked.

She hurried over to the sink to retrieve a damp cloth while the bishop flipped on a kerosene-powered lamp.

Seth dropped down onto the sofa. "I doubt it. I'll have to tell my attorney what happened. I have no idea what the judge might say. But it won't help the paternity case. Either I am Miriam's father, or I am not. We need this matter settled. But I don't want my *dochder* sent off to live in a foster home, either."

Susanna shuddered at the thought and handed the cloth to Seth. "Miriam can stay with *Mammi* and me for as long as needed. She never needs to leave. If it comes down to it, I will be her permanent foster mom."

Seth smiled and pressed the cool cloth against his nose and the side of his face. "*Danke*. I appreciate that, more than I can say. But I hope it doesn't *komm* to that." He looked at the bishop and tilted his head to one side in curiosity. "What brought the two of you here to my place this evening?"

Bishop Yoder shrugged. "I wanted an update on the paternity case. I stopped off at Susanna's farm first, then asked her to ride with me over here. I wondered if there had been any new developments and wanted to check on you, to see how you're holding up. I'm delighted by what I've found. You are a *gut*, strong man of faith, Seth. Now I believe the Lord must have been guiding me to *komm* here all along. He must have known you needed us this evening."

"*Ja*, He knows everything," Seth agreed.

Susanna must have looked worried because he smiled up at her with his reddened face. She had no doubt he'd have a nice bruise and some swelling by tomorrow morning.

"Stop worrying. I'm fine," he said.

He clasped his jaw and worked it back and forth, then wiggled his nose. "I don't think my nose is broken, thank the Lord. Rob rang my bell, though. My mind is feeling much clearer now."

The bishop exhaled a deep sigh, then glanced at Susanna. "*Ach*, I best take you *heemet* before it gets late. I don't want either of us out on these slick roads as the ice starts to freeze with the lower temperatures."

"*Ja*, you're right, of course." She turned toward the door.

The bishop followed, lifting a hand of farewell. *"Gut nacht."*

Seth nodded as he came to his feet. *"Vaarwel."*

She stepped out onto the landing with misgivings, then descended the stairs. Before she accompanied the bishop to his buggy, she ensured the outer door was locked up tight. If Rob returned that night, she didn't want him to have easy access to the building.

The ride to her farm didn't take long. The bishop didn't say much when he bid her farewell. He waited until she was safely inside her farmhouse before pulling away. She watched through the frosted windowpane as he urged his horse into a fast trot and drove onto the main road.

How she wished this paternity case was finished. She only hoped Seth was truly Miriam's father. Because the alternative was unthinkable. But once everything was resolved, where would that leave Susanna and Seth? Nowhere! Because no matter how much she adored that little baby and loved Seth, she wasn't tied to either of them in any way. The paternity case would be settled and they'd each move on with their lives. Seth had been Eve's husband, not hers. For all she knew, he only thought of them as friends, or friendly business partners. And the sooner Susanna accepted that, the better.

Chapter Thirteen

Three days before Christmas, it snowed in the night. A good three inches of white stuff blanketed the fields and craggy mountains surrounding the valley. It was heavy, wet stuff that would greatly increase their snowpack in the higher elevations and provide the all-important moisture they so desperately needed for their crops and gardens later in the summer months. Snow for Christmas was always a delight, too. And yet, Susanna couldn't feel happy about anything this morning. This was the day they would lose Miriam, and Susanna's heart ached with the thought of never seeing the little girl again.

Earlier, Seth had driven his horse and buggy over to Susanna's farm, to pick up her, *Mammi* and the baby so they wouldn't be late for their court appearance. All of them had bundled up nice and warm before they dropped *Mammi* off at the store. As always, the elderly woman would mind the noodle shop while Susanna was gone.

"It'll be a heavy shopping day with Christmas only a few days off. Are you sure you'll be *allrecht* here alone?" Susanna asked as she hugged her grandmother goodbye.

"*Ja*, I'll be fine, just as long as you bring this sweet little *hoppli* home safe where she belongs," *Mammi* said.

Seth stepped out of the buggy and walked around to open the carriage door. *Mammi* leaned forward and kissed Miriam's forehead, then caressed the child's soft cheek with her hand. As Seth took her arm to help her down, *Mammi* cast one last woeful look at Miriam. Strapped into her riding safety chair, the baby smiled with contentment and babbled in her happy voice, completely oblivious to the chaos going on around her.

Mammi's face contorted in an expression of sorrow and she looked as if she were about to burst into tears. Susanna bit her lip and turned away, knowing the woman's countenance mirrored how she felt inside. Even Seth had said very little that morning. Susanna waited inside the buggy with Miriam for several minutes, while Seth quickly shoveled the walkways to the store and spread ice melt so shoppers wouldn't fall on the slick paths. And when he was finished, *Mammi* waved from the doorway and blew them a kiss.

With ominous silence, Seth climbed back inside the buggy and drove them down the street to the city office building. The *whoosh* of the wheels turning in the slushy snow and the clip-clop of the horse's hooves were the only sounds. Without a word, he parked beneath a covered partition the town had built especially for the Amish in the area to use. As he set the brake, he stared out the windshield for several long moments, then blew out a heavy breath of resignation.

"*Ach*, we'd best go get this over with." Opening his door, he hopped down, then came around to help Susanna and the baby out of the conveyance.

Holding little Miriam in her arms, Susanna pressed her nose against the baby's warm cheek and breathed her in. She couldn't help wondering who would be looking after the child after today. Who would bathe and feed her and rock her to sleep with her favorite rag doll? Somehow, Susanna couldn't imagine Rob Thompson doing any of those things for Miriam. And the thought filled Susanna with absolute terror.

"I guess we'd better go inside now," Seth said, his voice roughened by emotion.

Yet, he made no move toward the building. Instead, he reached up and held Miriam's little hand, gazing at her sweet face as though he were drinking her in.

"Dat!" the baby said, reaching for him.

He didn't take her into his arms but he showed a sad little smile. And then, he said the words that Susanna had yearned for so long to hear from Thomas with every fiber of her being.

"I love you, little one. Please don't ever forget that."

Wiping at his eyes, Seth turned away. Susanna had to brush at her eyes as well.

She forced herself to push aside her doubts, hoping with all her might that some way, somehow they could take Miriam home with them again. She had to be strong. For Seth.

As they walked toward the building, Seth glanced at the baby, his reddened eyes filled with exhaustion and grief. None of them had been sleeping much. They were all too distracted with worry, yet determined to accept

Gott's will. Though he was a strong, hard-working man, Seth couldn't stop the court from taking his daughter from him, if that's what they decided to do. None of them could prevent this tragedy of justice. Only the Lord could help them now.

Susanna didn't flinch as Seth cupped her elbow with his hand to escort her up the icy sidewalk. She'd grown accustomed to his solicitous ways. And she loved him for it. Not once had he tried to impose his will upon her. He'd always asked rather than forcing her to do something she didn't want to do. Always thoughtful and caring. Even now, in times of trouble, Seth remained kind and deferential. The complete opposite of Thomas. And she was so grateful to Seth for teaching her that not all men were domineering and dictatorial. She loved him and Miriam with all her heart. But her love couldn't help them.

As they approached the building, it felt like they were heading toward their doom. Susanna offered another silent prayer for *Gott*'s assistance. As she faced the front door, she hugged Miriam tighter, fearing she might never see the tiny girl after today. Though she felt the grip of Seth's gentle hand on her arm through the fabric of her woolen shawl, he seemed so remote. Like he was walking to his execution. She didn't know what to say or how to comfort him.

"Seth, it's going to be *allrecht*. I just know it. We must believe that. We must have faith," she said, trying to convince herself, too.

Meeting her gaze, he nodded once as he held the front door open for her but he didn't speak. His pained expression spoke volumes.

They all stepped inside the warm city office building that housed the court. Seth doffed his black felt hat and held it in one hand. The small outer room smelled of cinnamon and clove air freshener. An imitation reminder of the coming Christmas holiday. But it was nothing like the real thing that filled Susanna's kitchen and home when she and *Mammi* baked fresh pumpkin bread.

Carl Nelson was there to greet them, dressed in his suit and tie and holding a battered briefcase. Rob Thompson's lawyer was there as well, sitting alone by himself. Rob was nowhere to be seen.

"Good morning! I was worried you might have trouble getting here through the snow. I was just about to drive over to your place in my car," Carl said.

"We left an hour earlier than usual, but my

horse is quite sure-footed. We arrived without incident," Seth said, his voice a low monotone.

Susanna nodded a greeting to Carl, then turned to one side of the room and sat alone with Miriam to wait. Seth moved away to speak with his attorney. Looking up, Susanna saw strands of artificial pine boughs and lights strung along the walls and front reception counter. A fake tree stood in one corner of the room, decorated with tinsel, lights and colorful balls of red, gold, blue and green. On the very top of the tree was an electric star, gleaming brightly. Several gaily wrapped packages with ostentatious bows rested on the floor.

Though the Amish didn't give lots of gifts or decorate with such flamboyant ornaments, they rejoiced in Jesus Christ's birth and always held a huge feast with happy visits among *familye* and friends. But this year, Susanna felt little joy. She and *Mammi* had no plans to go visiting anyone. Even Seth had declined her and *Mammi's* invitation to share Christmas dinner with them. He didn't need to explain why. Without Miriam to cheer up their empty homes, the last thing any of them wanted was to celebrate.

In her heart, Susanna felt as if she was losing more than just this baby. She was losing Seth, too. Her instincts told her that he needed her now more than ever. And yet, he seemed so distant and cold. He'd suffered more heartache than she could imagine. She didn't know how to reach him. She couldn't offer any words of condolence or comfort that would ease his pain. After today, he wouldn't be taking his meals with her and *Mammi*. Except for church and an occasional social gathering with their congregation, they'd be seeing very little of each other. No more haircuts or feeding the livestock with each other. No more laughing together over Miriam's cute little antics. There would be nothing left between them. With both of their histories, it was undoubtedly better this way. She didn't know if she could overcome her past with Thomas, even if Seth returned her affection. She wasn't sure his heart would ever be open to love after the grief of these months.

Other than *Mammi*, Susanna would live the rest of her days alone. It was for the best. After her tragic marriage to Thomas, she kept telling herself she didn't need any man in her life.

The doors to the improvised courtroom opened and Seth looked that way. A sinking feeling settled in his gut and he didn't want to go inside. At that moment, he wished he could hold back time. That he and Miriam could be anywhere but here.

If nothing else, he wanted to take his little daughter and Susanna outside, load them into his buggy and run away where he could keep them both safe forever more. But he knew that wasn't possible. He was only a man, after all. A man who believed in *Gott* and the Atonement of Jesus Christ. And right now, he must put his faith to the test. Without *Gott* and his religious beliefs, he was nothing. He'd done everything in his power to help Eve and to care for Miriam. Now, he must trust that the Lord knew what was best for them all and would take care of this situation.

He took a step, then stopped dead in his tracks. His courage almost failed him. And then, he felt a light touch and looked down. Susanna had reached up and cupped his upper arm with her hand. She gazed up at him, her eyes filled with compassion and concern. She held the baby with her free arm, standing close.

"It's going to be *allrecht*. I just know it," she said in *Deitsch*.

He stared into her eyes, almost lost in their

blue depths. For just a moment, he could almost believe what she said was true. Just looking at her and Miriam warmed his heart and renewed his faith. Though he was frightened of today's outcome, he felt an overwhelming love for both of them. How he wished they belonged to him. He didn't know how or where this love came from, but it buoyed him up and gave him the confidence to face whatever was to come.

"Let's go on in," Carl Nelson said, lifting a hand toward the open doorway.

Seth blinked, as though awakened from a dream. And then, he made a determination to exercise his faith. He knew his Savior loved him. He knew *Gott* was fully aware of what he was going through. And somehow, he would get through this and there would be happy days ahead. He had to feed off Susanna's words and trust in the Lord. Because that's all he had left.

He nodded at Carl, then took the heavy diaper bag from Susanna and waited for her to precede him into the courtroom. Bill Griffin, the lawyer representing Rob Thompson, followed behind them. But where was Rob? It was time for the judge to read the paternity results, yet the man still hadn't made an appearance.

Like the last time they were here, the bailiff greeted them all and indicated that Susanna should sit in the back spectator area. After she'd taken a seat, Seth placed the diaper bag beside her on the floor. Carl went up to the front and laid his black briefcase on the table.

Helping Susanna remove all the bulky winter clothes from the baby, Seth pulled her gray knit cap from off her head. It revealed the starched, white prayer *kapp* Susanna had made for her weeks earlier. Susanna was always thoughtful that way. She made such a great mother.

Once they were settled, Seth gazed into his child's big blue eyes and smiled. Oh, how he loved her! No matter what, she would always belong to him. He didn't need a paternity test to tell him that he was her daddy. She would always be the child of his heart.

He glanced at Susanna and another surge of love washed over him. This woman had selflessly taught him so many lessons about compassion and caring. His only Christmas wish was that he and Susanna could take Miriam home and be a *familye* for real. If *Gott* would grant him this one heart's desire, he would never ask for anything more.

"You'd better go on now. Carl is waiting

for you," Susanna said, jutting her chin toward the attorney.

Seth looked up and saw that Bill Griffin was already sitting in his seat, staring straight ahead as he waited quietly for the judge to appear. The bailiff closed the outer door before stationing herself beside the front dais. But where was Rob? Why wasn't the guy here yet?

Turning, Seth stepped over to the vacant chair beside Carl and sat down. Within moments, the door leading to the judge's chamber opened and the bailiff called out in a loud, clear voice.

"The Honorable Clinton Cook presiding."

They all stood as the judge stepped up to his desk and sat down.

Here we go again! Seth couldn't stop hoping that Rob had withdrawn his petition and they could all go home now and forget this awful paternity case.

Looking out at the courtroom, the judge waved a hand at the occupants. "Be seated."

They did as instructed and the judge reached for a rather large, official-looking manila envelope sitting on his desk.

Looking up, Judge Cook glanced first at Seth, then over at Bill. "Mr. Griffin, where is your client today?"

Bill scooted back his seat and stood as he addressed the judge. "I'm sorry, Your Honor, but Mr. Thompson is unfortunately indisposed today."

The judge gave a surprised little jerk of his head that indicated he was irritated by this explanation. Then, he frowned. "Indisposed? What exactly do you mean?"

Bill gave a little shrug of reticence and looked down, as if he didn't want to explain. "He's in the hospital, Your Honor."

Judge Cook leaned forward and rested one elbow on the desk. "I hope it isn't serious. For what reason is Mr. Thompson in the hospital?"

The attorney cleared his throat and shifted his feet in a moment of discomfort. "He... um, had a drug overdose yesterday and was admitted to the hospital in the middle of the night. I would ask for the court's leniency. If we could have a few extra days, then Mr. Thompson could be present for this hearing."

Seth held his breath, wondering what would happen now. He'd been on pins and needles for several weeks already. He wanted this case dealt with now so he could be put out of his misery. With Rob out of commission, who would take Miriam once the paternity tests determined that he was her biological father? Would the judge let Miriam go home with Susanna until Rob was well enough to take her? Seth hated to ask that of Susanna. Already, the baby had been sleeping over at her house each night. Seth could only see his daughter when Susanna was in the room. This delay wasn't fair to any of them. Though Susanna had been tending Miriam like she was her own daughter, Seth had imposed on her long enough. He didn't know if he could take much more of this, either. The fretting and anguish. The not knowing.

Carl came to his feet and held out a pleading hand. "Your Honor, Mr. Thompson knew the importance of this court date. It isn't my client's fault that Mr. Thompson has a drug problem and overdosed. Mr. Lehman has been more than patient during this trying time. Since the child in question was born, Mr. Lehman has believed she was his own true daughter and he deserves to know the final results right now."

Judge Cook heaved a disgruntled sigh, then sat back in his chair and tilted his head to one side as he thought this over. "I agree. To wait until Mr. Thompson has his act together would delay this hearing another three weeks, until this court is back in session. It's Christmastime and I think we've already put Mr. Lehman through enough suffering as it is. We have the results of the paternity tests here on my desk and we will proceed with the announcement of the findings today. Depending on that outcome, this court will then decide what should happen with the child in question."

"But, Your Honor..." Bill began.

"Mr. Griffin, be seated." A flash of fire filled Judge Cook's eyes and he spoke in a low but slaying tone.

Bill sat down, his jaw locked hard as he stared at the judge and folded his hands in his lap. He obviously didn't like the judge's decision but he had no choice but to accept it.

Having established order in his court, Judge Cook reached for a letter opener and the manila envelope. As he slit the top open and removed the contents, Seth realized even the judge didn't know the results yet.

Seth sat still as stone, unable to move. Unable to breathe. He clenched his hands tightly in fists and waited. In the quiet room, he could hear the clock on the wall, ticking off each tense second as the judge scanned the page in front of him.

With Rob absent today, what would the judge do with Miriam? Would he let Susanna keep the baby until Rob was out of the hospital? Would the judge schedule a date when they must hand over the baby and all her little clothes? Or maybe Rob had family members who could look after the child. Maybe she would even be sent to stay with a foster family.

Seth could hardly stand the thought of any of these outcomes. It wasn't right. It wasn't fair. Miriam deserved to go home with him, where she belonged.

The judge laid the paper on his desk and removed his spectacles to set them aside. Then, he leaned forward and gazed intently at Seth. And suddenly, a wide smile spread its way across the older man's face.

"Mr. Lehman, I am very relieved and quite pleased to announce that you are the father of this child. The paternity tests were 99.9 percent conclusive in your favor. You are free to take your daughter home with you right now and I wish you both a long and happy life. Merry Christmas!"

With that last statement, the judge picked up his gavel and brought it down hard in finality.

A small cry of joy came from behind Seth and he thought it must have come from Susanna. He stared at the judge for several long moments, unable to absorb what he had said. Seth dropped his mouth open in absolute shock, trying to take it all in. Trying to accept the truth.

Miriam was his daughter? He was her biological father! The tests couldn't be wrong, could they? No! It was biology, after all. Scientific facts didn't care about what was right and wrong.

"Congratulations!" Carl hooted in victory, then turned toward Seth and took his hand, pumping it up and down like a water handle. A smile of delight spread across the man's face and he laughed out loud.

Somehow, Seth found himself standing. He blew out an exhale of relief and smiled at his attorney. Miriam was really his. He couldn't believe it.

He turned to find his daughter and Susanna and nearly fell over the top of them. With a smile of absolute joy on her face, Susanna thrust the baby into his arms.

"Here, she is yours. I think you will want to hold your *dochder* for a very long while," she said, speaking in *Deitsch*.

He laughed deeply, feeling so much happiness that he couldn't contain it for a moment. "You are right about that. I want to hold her and never let her go."

He cradled his little girl close to his chest for several long minutes, burying his face against her tiny shoulder. She chortled and tugged his hair, seeming to understand how jubilant this moment was. He kissed her cheek and forehead, breathing in her fragrant scent of baby lotion that Susanna must have rubbed all over her earlier that morning. Oh, how he loved this baby. How he loved Susanna.

"Daedi!" Miriam said, patting his head with the flat of her hands.

Lifting his face to her, he gently untwined her fingers from his hair and laughed.

"She's really got a hold on you," Susanna said, her gaze filled with approval and adoration as she gazed at Miriam.

"Ja, she sure does. And now, I've got a firm hold on her, too." Tears burned the backs of Seth's eyes and he was almost overcome by emotion. He couldn't believe this was happening. He tried not to second-guess it and just enjoy this sweet, blessed moment with his baby and Susanna.

"I still don't know how I could be her biological father," he spoke low in *Deitsch* to Susanna, so no one else would understand.

She shrugged, cupping one of Miriam's little hands with her own. "Eve's dates must have been wrong. It's that's simple."

Was it? Yes, that was the only reasonable explanation. The dates had never lined up quite right. Eve must have been farther along than she realized and Miriam was born late. It didn't matter now. The judge had read the paternity results. He had rendered his final judgment. Miriam was Seth's and he was hers. And the only thing that would make the Christmas holiday better was if Susanna…

"Well, that's it for me. I'm headed back to my office." Carl came over to them and clapped Seth on the back, still grinning like a fool.

No doubt the lawyer felt good to have won this case. But he could never feel as good as Seth did at that point in time. Seth nodded, his face hurting from smiling so much.

"Thank you, Carl. Thank you so much. I don't know how to ever repay you," he said.

Carl chuckled. "You're welcome. And don't worry. I'll send you my final bill and the paperwork in the mail, along with the court's ruling."

Seth just nodded with ready acceptance. That was one bill he would gladly pay. It had been worth every penny he owned just to put this issue to an end. To know in his heart that he was truly Miriam's father for real.

Carl nodded to him and then Susanna. "You two have yourself a very merry Christmas."

"You know we will," Seth said.

Susanna waved and her sweet voice filled the air. "And merry Christmas to you, too."

As Seth turned toward her, he noticed they were alone in the room. Rob's attorney had disappeared, no doubt running back to his office, where he could be alone after such a loss.

Seth gazed into Susanna's eyes, feeling spellbound by her beauty. And suddenly, it was just him and Susanna. No one else existed in the whole wide world. Not even little Miriam. A heavy feeling settled in his chest. There were so many things he wanted to say to her. So many emotions he had to convey. But just now, alone like this with her and Miriam, he felt unexpectedly tongue-tied.

Chapter Fourteen

❧

Susanna forced herself to look away from Seth. His smile and deep voice made her feel all warm and mushy inside. For a few moments, she'd let down her guard. But she didn't want to be hurt. Never again. Her freedom and independence were all-important to her. Now that the paternity case was settled, Miriam was safely where she belonged. With a father who loved her. After next week, she would be going over to Ruth Lapp's home to receive childcare while Seth worked his farm. Susanna wouldn't be seeing much of the baby, or her enigmatic father. And that's what Susanna wanted. In spite of her love for both of them, it was best this way. Wasn't it?

"I hope this court case wasn't too hard on you," Seth said, taking a step closer.

"*Ne*, of course not. Don't be silly. There's

very little I wouldn't do for this little girl. I love her," she said with a slight laugh, reaching out to brush her fingertips against Miriam's arm.

"*Gut!* I'm so glad to hear that."

"I'm hoping after today, you'll change your mind about joining *Mammi* and me for Christmas dinner," she said.

He nodded. "I'd like that very much. We have a lot to celebrate."

"*Ja*, we sure do," she agreed.

Seth stepped closer and she lifted her head to look up at him. He raised a hand and brushed his fingertips against her cheek. A tingly sensation rushed over her and she shivered. What was he doing?

She took a step back, feeling suddenly awkward. "I don't know what could make this day more perfect."

"I can think of one thing." He spoke low, closing the distance between them.

"You can?" she asked.

He nodded, holding her gaze captive with his. Susanna would have stepped away, but her back bumped against the wall. There was nowhere for her to go, except around him and Miriam.

"Seth, I…"

"I know you need to get back to the noodle

store. Dorothy is alone and it's a busy time for you. But I was hoping to detain you just a few minutes more. You see, there's something vitally important that I need to discuss with you," he said.

She stared up at him, feeling mesmerized by the golden specks in his hazel eyes. "There is?"

"*Ja*, there is. You see, I've fallen madly in love with you, Susanna. During the most difficult time of my life, you've been there like a rock. Supportive and unflinching. Always compassionate and caring. Never judgmental. I've never met another woman like you in the whole wide world. And I'd be honored if you would agree to marry me. Your agreement is what would make this day even better. It would fulfill my Christmas wish."

A little breath of air escaped her lungs and she felt overwhelmed by his declaration. She was his Christmas wish? She could hardly believe it.

"Seth, I don't know…"

"Susanna," he cut her off with a gentle, yet insistent voice. "Before you say anything, I want you to know that, over the past few months, you've given me a glimpse of what a healthy, happy marriage could be like. I can't imagine raising Miriam without you."

"You... You can't?" She felt nervous and jittery, like she'd swallowed bees. A part of her wanted to run from the room. Another part felt exhilarated and so happy that she didn't know what to say.

"*Ne*, I can't. I understand what you went through with Thomas. I think you know me well enough by now that you realize I would never treat you the way he did. And I promise here and now, I'll never take away your independence, either. I'm stunned by all you've accomplished. You set up your own noodle shop. You're amazing and wonderful. I would never take that away from you. I'm so pleased with you. All I'm asking is that you let Miriam and me share your life. And maybe one day, we could have more children together. But if that isn't possible, I just want you. You, Miriam and the Lord are all that matter to me now."

Before she could respond, he got down on one knee. Still holding Miriam with one arm, he reached out and took Susanna's hand in his. Turning her palm upward, he placed a very slow, very gentle kiss there.

He looked up into her eyes. "Susanna Glick, I love you. Please say you'll marry me and make me the happiest man in the world."

Susanna couldn't believe what she was

hearing. "Do you really mean it, Seth? You really love me?"

He nodded and released a light chuckle. "I do. With all my heart."

She pulled him up and into her arms. As they embraced, they squeezed Miriam between them.

"I… I love you, too," Susanna confessed on a slight whisper. But once she'd said the words, they gave her courage and she said them again, louder this time. "*Ja*, I love you, Seth. So very much. For the longest time, I thought remaining single was the best thing for me. After what I suffered at the hands of Thomas, I never thought I could trust another man again. But you've taught me that isn't true. You've been nothing but steadfast and kind, no matter what life threw at you. And I realize, I want nothing more than to marry you and raise a *familye* of my own. With you. You've helped me gain the courage to take another leap of faith and I really am ready to put my trust in you and the Lord."

As she said these things, she understood deep in her heart that she meant all of it. Suddenly, there was nothing left to say. She was in his arms and he kissed her. Loving and passionately. And when he finally released her, he smiled into her eyes.

"*Komm* on. Let's go home," he said.

She laughed, linking her arm with his. "Is that to my house, or your apartment? Where is *heemet* for us, Seth?"

"My *heemet* is with you, Susanna. That's all that matters to me. I'll let you and *Mammi* decide where we're all going to live."

As they walked out of the courtroom and into the cold air, Susanna felt perfectly happy with his response. After donning their warm winter garb, they stepped out onto the front steps. It had started to snow and little Miriam babbled with delight. Her cute, high-pitched giggle made each of them laugh. They headed down the walk path, buoyed by their new-found love as they made plans to be married as soon as possible. After all, they had their whole lives ahead of them and they wanted to build it together.

Gone were Susanna's misgivings. She had no more doubts or fears. Her greatest wish for this Christmas season had just been fulfilled. Their faith and trust in *Gott*'s redeeming love had overcome all. And she couldn't ask for anything more.

* * * * *

*If you enjoyed this
Secret Amish Babies story,
be sure to pick up these previous books
in Leigh Bale's miniseries:*

The Midwife's Christmas Wish
Her Forbidden Amish Child

Available now from Love Inspired!

Dear Reader,

Have you ever had your heart broken or suffered abuse from someone you cared about through no fault of your own? In this story, Susanna Glick is the widow of an abusive husband. And Seth Lehman's deceased wife was addicted to illicit drugs. Both Susanna and Seth have suffered broken hearts. Both struggle with feelings of guilt because they weren't able to help their spouses and are relieved they are gone, yet they also long for the healing power of forgiveness. And though it takes some time, they finally learn the liberating lesson that forgiveness can change bitterness to love.

Thanks to the Atonement of Jesus Christ, every hurt we suffer in this life can be healed. No matter how small or large, the wounds we suffer can be made whole because our Savior has already paid the price to make them right. Forgiveness doesn't mean we excuse the sin or waive its consequences. It simply means we turn judgment and payment for that sin over to God. It's not always easy to forgive and heal. It can definitely be an arduous process. But if we will hand our burdens over to our Savior and turn and follow Him, we can be made whole and freed from the misery of anger and guilt.

I hope you enjoyed reading this story and I invite you to visit my website at www.Leigh-Bale.com to learn more about my books.

May you find peace in the Lord's words!

Leigh Bale

Get 4 FREE REWARDS!

We'll send you 2 FREE Books plus 2 FREE Mystery Gifts.

FREE
Value Over
$20

Both the **Love Inspired®** and **Love Inspired® Suspense** series feature compelling novels filled with inspirational romance, faith, forgiveness, and hope.

Get 4 FREE REWARDS!

We'll send you 2 FREE Books <u>plus</u> 2 FREE Mystery Gifts.

FREE
Value Over
$20

Both the **Harlequin® Special Edition** and **Harlequin® Heartwarming™** series feature compelling novels filled with stories of love and strength where the bonds of friendship, family and community unite.

YES! Please send me 2 FREE novels from the Harlequin Special Edition or Harlequin Heartwarming series and my 2 FREE gifts (gifts are worth about $10 retail). After receiving them, if I don't wish to receive any more books, I can return the shipping statement marked "cancel." If I don't cancel, I will receive 6 brand-new Harlequin Special Edition books every month and be billed just $5.24 each in the U.S. or $5.99 each in Canada, a savings of at least 13% off the cover price or 4 brand-new Harlequin Heartwarming Larger-Print books every month and be billed just $5.99 each in the U.S. or $6.49 each in Canada, a savings of at least 20% off the cover price. It's quite a bargain! Shipping and handling is just 50¢ per book in the U.S. and $1.25 per book in Canada.* I understand that accepting the 2 free books and gifts places me under no obligation to buy anything. I can always return a shipment and cancel at any time by calling the number below. The free books and gifts are mine to keep no matter what I decide.

Choose one: ☐ **Harlequin Special Edition**   ☐ **Harlequin Heartwarming**
                    (235/335 HDN GRCQ)   **Larger-Print**
                                                                          (161/361 HDN GRC3)

Name (please print)

Address   Apt. #

City   State/Province   Zip/Postal Code

Email: Please check this box ☐ if you would like to receive newsletters and promotional emails from Harlequin Enterprises ULC and its affiliates. You can unsubscribe anytime.

> **Mail to the Harlequin Reader Service:**
> **IN U.S.A.:** P.O. Box 1341, Buffalo, NY 14240-8531
> **IN CANADA:** P.O. Box 603, Fort Erie, Ontario L2A 5X3

Want to try 2 free books from another series! Call 1-800-873-8635 or visit www.ReaderService.com.

---

*Terms and prices subject to change without notice. Prices do not include sales taxes, which will be charged (if applicable) based on your state or country of residence. Canadian residents will be charged applicable taxes. Offer not valid in Quebec. This offer is limited to one order per household. Books received may not be as shown. Not valid for current subscribers to the Harlequin Special Edition or Harlequin Heartwarming series. All orders subject to approval. Credit or debit balances in a customer's account(s) may be offset by any other outstanding balance owed by or to the customer. Please allow 4 to 6 weeks for delivery. Offer available while quantities last.

Your Privacy—Your information is being collected by Harlequin Enterprises ULC, operating as Harlequin Reader Service. For a complete summary of the information we collect, how we use this information and to whom it is disclosed, please visit our privacy notice located at corporate.harlequin.com/privacy-notice. From time to time we may also exchange your personal information with reputable third parties. If you wish to opt out of this sharing of your personal information, please visit readerservice.com/consumerschoice or call 1 800 873-8635 **Notice to California Residents**—Under California law, you have specific rights to control and access your data. For more information on these rights and how to exercise them, visit corporate.harlequin.com/california-privacy.

HSEHW22R2

THE 2022 LOVE INSPIRED CHRISTMAS COLLECTION

Buy 3 and get 1 FREE!

May all that is beautiful, meaningful and brings you joy be yours this holiday season...including this fun-filled collection featuring 24 Christmas stories. From tender holiday romances to Christmas Eve suspense, this collection has it all.

YES! Please send me the **2022 LOVE INSPIRED CHRISTMAS COLLECTION** in Larger Print! This collection begins with ONE FREE book and 2 FREE gifts in the first shipment. Along with my FREE book, I'll get another 3 Larger Print books! If I do not cancel, I will continue to receive four books a month for five more months. Each shipment will contain another FREE gift. I'll pay just $23.97 U.S./$26.97 CAN., plus $1.99 U.S./$4.99 CAN. for shipping and handling per shipment.* I understand that accepting the free books and gifts places me under no obligation to buy anything. I can always return a shipment and cancel at any time. My free books and gifts are mine to keep no matter what I decide.

☐ 298 HCK 0958   ☐ 498 HCK 0958

Name (please print)

Address   Apt. #

City   State/Province   Zip/Postal Code

Mail to the Harlequin Reader Service:
IN U.S.A.: P.O. Box 1341, Buffalo, NY 14240-8531
IN CANADA: P.O. Box 603, Fort Erie, ON L2A 5X3

COMING NEXT MONTH FROM
Love Inspired

HER UNLIKELY AMISH PROTECTOR
by Jocelyn McClay
Amish nanny Miriam Schrock isn't pleased when handsome bad boy Aaron Raber starts working for the same family as she does. But soon Miriam sees the good man he's become. When his troubled past threatens them both, Aaron must step in to protect the only one who truly believes in him...

THE MYSTERIOUS AMISH NANNY
by Patrice Lewis
Lonely Amish widower Adam Chupp needs help raising his young son. When outsider Ruth Wengerd's car breaks down, she agrees to care for Lucas until it can be repaired. Ruth fits into Amish life easily but is secretive about her past. Will Adam learn the truth about her before he loses his heart?

RESTORING THEIR FAMILY
True North Springs • by Allie Pleiter
Widow Kate Hoyle arrives at Camp True North Springs to heal her grieving family, not the problems of camp chef Seb Costa. But the connection the bold-hearted chef makes with her son—and with her own heart—creates a recipe for love and hope neither one of them expects.

THE BABY PROPOSAL
by Gabrielle Meyer
After his brother's death, Drew Keelan finds himself guardian of his infant nephew. But to keep custody, Drew must get married fast! He proposes a marriage in name only to the baby's aunt, Whitney Emmerson. But when things get complicated, will love help keep their marriage going?

RECLAIMING THE RANCHER'S HEART
by Lisa Carter
Rancher Jack Dolan is surprised when his ex-wife, Kate, returns to town and tells him that they are still married. He suggests that they honor the memory of their late daughter one last time, then go their separate ways. This could be the path to healing—and finding their way back to each other...

THE LONER'S SECRET PAST
by Lorraine Beatty
Eager for a fresh start, single mom Sara Holden comes to Mississippi to help redo her sister's antique shop. And she needs local contractor Luke McBride's help. But the gruff, unfriendly man wants nothing to do with Sara. Can she convince him to come out of seclusion and back to life?

LOOK FOR THESE AND OTHER LOVE INSPIRED BOOKS WHEREVER BOOKS ARE SOLD, INCLUDING MOST BOOKSTORES, SUPERMARKETS, DISCOUNT STORES AND DRUGSTORES.

LICNM1122